I0623232

The New Players:
Origins

Players of the Game: Book 3.5
James McGowan

Copyright ©2020-2022 by James McGowan

All rights reserved. No part of this book may be reproduced without written permission, except for brief quotations to books and critical reviews. This story is a work of fiction. Characters and events are the product of the author's imagination. Any resemblance to persons, living or dead, is purely coincidental.

CONTENTS

THE NEW PLAYERS: ORIGINS

Players of the Game: Book 3.5

A Novella by James McGowan

©2020-2022 by James McGowan

Published 2022 by James McGowan

Edited by Sarah Buhrman

Cover by Mikhail Palamarchuk

Cover Design by Tony McGowan

Maps by Tony McGowan and James McGowan

Website: stelfire.com

Facebook Fan Page: JamesMcGowanAuthor

Join the James McGowan Reader Group at stelfire.com

Get a notification email for all new releases in the series at https://books2r
ead.com/author/james-mcgowan/subscribe/1/174474/

All rights reserved. No part of this book may be reproduced without written permission, except for brief quotations to books and critical reviews. This story is a work of fiction. Characters and events are the product of the author's imagination. Any resemblance to persons, living or dead, is purely coincidental.

JOIN THE JAMES McGOWAN READER GROUP!

Go to stelfire.comor use the QR code above to join James McGowan's Reader Group to receive the monthly newsletter. Get the latest missives on works in progress, novel and comic book recommendations, video game and movie obsessions, along with character profiles and fantastic artwork.

Acknowledgments

Thanks and eternal love to my wife, Steph, who never stopped encouraging and supporting me as I scratch this writing itch.

FOREWORD

This novel takes place prior to the events of the New Players main novel. It can be read either before or after the main novel.

DEDICATION

This novella is dedicated to the memory of my grandfather, Gene Nielsen. A man of dry wit and cowboy grit.

PLAYERS OF THE GAME SERIES

TROJISI CALENDAR

The Trojisi year has 389 days, each lasting 24 hours. The following bi-months comprise the calendar:

1) Pyrene: 63 days.

2) Blite: 67 days.

3) Trires: 64 days.

4) Quatres: 65 days.

5) Quintember: 65 days.

6) Hexember: 65 days.

The ambient etherea in Trojis, Sufrinzon, and their related realms extends all mortal life by a factor of six percent.

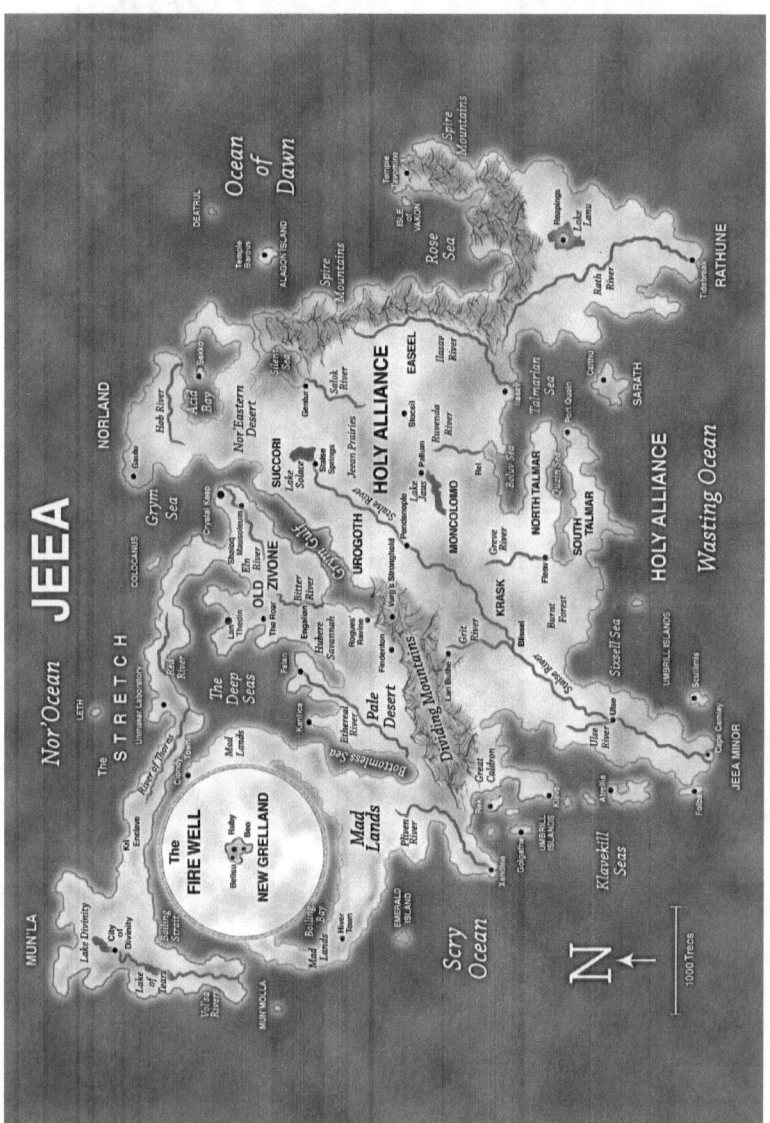

PART I: GATHINER

CHAPTER 1

"My wife betrayed us. I killed her, but not for that." Rick Burnhelt clenched his fingers against his rifle's grip. "I still love her."

Gath glanced up at his taller friend, then back to the shimmering phenomenon fifty feet in front of them. "Really? Two years of me asking you to tell me what happened, and you choose now? Out of nowhere? In the middle of this shit storm?"

"A day before." Rick cleared his throat, plainly forcing himself to utter something bitter. "A day before the rest of it, Cora told me about portals that looked like broken mirrors suspended in effervescent water."

He nodded to the churning, twinkling space beyond them. It did indeed look as the dead woman had described. "She and Corsis encountered something that came out of it. She never told me exactly what. Neither did he. These portals. She went bad because of them."

Gath chose silence rather than another reply. He checked the red graphical readout against the black display on his wrist computer. The device chirped out a high-pitched warning tone, signifying activity on the other side.

This portal thankfully didn't manifest in another city like the others. Too many people had lost their lives already. This place was isolated. The vacant hills spanned in all directions. Wind ruffled through the knee-high, tan grass, carrying a scent of rain. Clouds churned in the overcast sky, dumping vast smears of indigo-hued precipitation near the horizon. The danger here threatened only the pair of men who dared to confront it.

"Say something, Gath." Rick maintained his parlesto rifle's aim at the anomaly. Light glowed along the sides of its lengthy, grey barrel, illuminating his brown hair and gray temples. The old soldier remained spry, always ready to act. Gath often found it difficult to believe that Rick was fifty-eight.

Gath took a few more seconds to choose his words. "She tried to raze Zandris with an army of Demons. That seems like a damn good reason to kill her to me." The shorter man ran his hand down his well-trimmed, bristly beard. "So if it wasn't her betrayal, why did you do it?"

"I impaled her through the throat." Rick's body tensed. His hard, angular face rarely showed weariness. It did now. "I did it because she told me she was going to kill our son at noon that day. Eat his eyes, then his heart."

Gath raised an eyebrow. "Ben or Veloc?"

"Ben."

The bearded man took a step beyond Rick. He pulled out a baton-like device from his belt, a mancy meter. It measured ethereal energy outside of the electromagnetic spectrum. "She woulda failed."

The old soldier remained quiet while Gath pointed the mancy meter at the fractured illumination. Rick reached into a sleeve pocket in his blue and black combat fatigues. "You didn't see her. What she did before I kicked down the door. I saved my eldest child. Believe me."

The mancy meter screeched out a shrill chime. As did Gath's wrist computer. "It's going hot. Like the others. Get ready."

"Then put away the toy." Rick brushed the back of his thumb against the hard, grey carbon of his vest armor.

The younger, bearded man replaced the mancy detector with his snub-nosed om pistol from his hip holster. "We should have a gods damned battalion backing us up."

"From where? The syndicates don't have anyone to spare." The old soldier looked at the trembling air through his rifle's scope. He then checked the sleek vamberg sword sheathed at his side. "I'm just happy they assigned me a mechmancer."

Gath snorted. "Like I woulda let you come here alone."

The shimmering matter doubled in size. The short man pressed two tiny buttons on his wrist computer. "*Field of Quandric.*" The device's synthesized voice spoke the hexing phrase in a passionless monotone.

A transparent dome wavered into existence around them as a lithe, pale, feminine arm reached out of the undulating, lustrous space in front of them. A naked woman emerged from the portal. Opposite skin tones symmetrically divided her statuesque body down the center, pitch-black on the left side, chalk-white on the right. Eerie grey flames burned atop her bald head, reminiscent of wild, billowing hair. The same dingy fire burned within her eyes.

"Hold your fire." Rick's jaw tightened as he whispered to himself. "Cora. You weren't lying."

"The Divided Woman." Gath said her name in a gasp. He pressed two buttons on the top edges of his wrist computer, diverting more ethereal power to the energy field surrounding them. A countdown also began. They had thirty-eight seconds from her arrival to tell her something she wanted to hear or face her attack. Only Corsis had answered the woman's random questions to her satisfaction. No one else survived an encounter with this female entity.

"Tell me your name, little timekeeper?" She spoke in a clear but soft voice.

"Gathiner of Haven Isle," the mechmancer immediately said. Twenty-nine seconds remained.

"You disinterest me." She tilted her head at twenty-three seconds. "Your ally does not." The woman's soulless, burning eyes stared at Rick. "My search is over, Rick Burnhelt. You are the love Cora of Transvahlu."

Rick gave Gath a quick glance at seventeen seconds. His finger twitched closer to the rifle's trigger.

The Divided Woman pointed at the old soldier with a rigid arm. "I turned her. You lost her because of me." With twelve seconds left, a faint smile crossed her lips. "Thank me."

Gath looked at his friend's icy-blue eyes as he beheld her. Five more seconds passed. Rick at last asked, "How?"

"Interesting response." The dust-hued fire in her ocular cavities intensified. "But not the right one. Thank me with your screams."

Rick gnashed his teeth as the timer hit zero. Both the old soldier and the mechmancer dove to the grass while firing their guns. Rick's red beam struck her in the neck. Gath's blue beam flecked with silvery particles went wide. A shockwave of grey fire surged from her pointed finger over everything in a blazing cone, incinerating the grass. The Field of Quandric quivered against the inferno, but it held as everything around them burned. No heat permeated the shield at all.

From his stomach, the old soldier fired at her again, this time hitting her between the eyes. Gath also scored a hit on her abdomen. Both the parlesto rifle and om pistol had enough firepower to penetrate a foot of carbon armor. Only singed blemishes marred her alabaster and onyx-hued skin.

Rick unsheathed his vamberg sword. Its silver, straight blade glimmered against the eerie fire's light. The weapon carried far greater threat than any gun. Its outer edge measured a single atom in width. Nothing was sharper. "Kill the flames."

"Workin' on it." Gath reached into a pocket on his jacket's shoulder and grabbed a knuckle-sized, glossy-black coin. He squeezed it and its hue changed to transparent blue. Another monotone, artificial voice spoke from the tiny device. "*Negate Mancy.*"

The dingy flare intensified, completely engulfing everything around the protective dome. The Divided Woman still lurked beyond the blaze, though they could not see her. Cracks ran along the Field of Quandric's interior. Gath's wrist computer blared out an alarm. Only seconds remained before the inferno consumed them.

Gath tossed the device while holding his breath. The chances of suppressing this entity's innate ethereal energy fell just short of twenty percent. The glassy coin passed through the dome's threshold into the fire and disintegrated. Her flames extinguished with an instant whoosh of air. The female entity beheld them with hollow eyes. Smoke rose from her bald head and the rest of the blasted hill.

"Hell fuckin' yeah!" A wave of elated relief flooded through the mechmancer. He flipped a switch on the side of the om pistol. The grey, snub-nosed barrel telescoped outward with a metallic snap, quintupling its length. He hoped gravity pulses had more effect than proton beams.

Rick sprinted toward their foe. He fired the parlesto rifle in controlled but unaimed bursts. Those blasts that hit her did nothing to her. She moved her finger in Rick's direction.

Before she could act, Gath moved to the side and shot out a colorless, marble-sized sphere at her face. The concussion of the gravity pulse's impact knocked her back a step as Rick reached her. The vamberg sliced off her head with a precise swipe. She fell to her knees as her head hit the charred earth at her side. Her body slumped down. Nothing bled. No organs or ichor filled the empty interior of both her cranium and her torso.

Rick cocked an eyebrow. "She's hollow."

"And she may not be solo." Gath looked at the glimmering space just beyond his friend's position. "I need to figure out how to close it fast."

"We need to talk to Corsis when this is over. Find out what he knows." The old soldier nudged her cheek with his boot. An unholy hiss escaped her lips. Rick leapt back. "She's alive!"

A grey flare burst out of her body atop her severed neck as it stood to its feet. Fire filled the Divided Woman's empty eyes. Her head levitated from the ground, propelled by a blazing vent. Rick tried slicing her face, but the atomically sharp blade glanced off her white and black skin. Gath shot more spherical pulses at both parts of her. All of them deflected skyward.

The female entity smiled with malevolence when her head reconnected, containing the inferno within her hollow form. "Thank me, Rick."

"Thank you," a gravelly voice said from behind her within the portal. A metal being leapt from the churning space, a robot of bizarre design. It landed behind her with a jolt of the earth, standing seven feet tall. Cylindrical arms and legs moved with deft agility. It walked on feet that ended in a sharp point at the front, like the tips of wrangler boots. A zigzagging metal visor was riveted to its face in place of its eyes. An exaggerated, silver-toothed grin carried both mirth and menace.

The Divided Woman's prior arrogant contentment drained from her face. Shock replaced it. "Xax."

The robot took a step toward her. "Eavae, you gotta stop."

Gath kept his weapon pointed at the woman rather than the mechanical newcomer as he flipped two switches at its rear. Rick dashed to the side. "Do it!"

The om pistol shot an icy blast of pale blue energy that pounded into her chest, instantly crystallizing the air around her in a jagged, frigid coating. Her body temperature lowered to absolute zero from the heat siphon beam's influence, halting all molecular activity.

The robot, Xax, looked in Gath's direction. Its mouth did not move when it spoke. "Eavae adapts. Ease off the freezification, gadgety guy. Let me take a whack."

Gath glanced at a readout on the back of his weapon. Her internal heat rose despite the physical impossibility of such a feat. She would break free in seconds. The mechmancer released the trigger, and the beam ceased. "Give it room, Rick."

The old soldier took a few more steps back, gripping his rifle in one hand and his sword in the other.

"Room," Xax said. "Great idea. Let's make some." The robot slammed its—no, his chrome fists together with a metallic ring. Glowing cones of white energy surrounded his hands with a crackling hiss. He punched through her chest and out her back as the ice evaporated from her skin.

The smirk returned to her face. "You're losing the Game, defender. We've evolved beyond you."

Grey flames flared around the Divided Woman, Eavae, and Xax in erratic, jagged patterns like electricity. He tried hitting her with his free hand's energy cone, but she deflected it with a slice of her palm. The surge of electric fire intensified. The robot convulsed while trying to pull away from her. He remained ensnared.

Rick looked at the undulating tear in reality, then back to the two grappling strangers. "Gath, figure out a way to close the portal. You were right. She isn't alone."

The taller man fired the parlesto rifle with wild abandon at the shimmering threshold. Gath had no idea what Rick saw. It didn't matter. This had to end.

The mechmancer ran his finger along the wrist computer's display. His eyes widened. Bizarre code scrolled across it in gold symbols. The indecipherable text moved on to a single word in Grellish: Close. The robot uploaded a hex into his system. A raindrop splattered against the device.

Gath pressed the button on the side. The churning portal quivered for a second. Its mirror-like liquid then imploded on itself with a deafening pop.

Eavae's crackling dust-colored energy immediately ceased. Xax fell on his back with a thud, motionless. The female entity's dingy fire diminished, but it still burned. She turned to Gath with her face twisted in fury, a gaping hole in her chest ablaze. She pointed her burning hand at him. "Now, you interest me."

From behind, Rick sliced off her arm at the elbow. A flare burst skyward from the wound. The severed appendage disintegrated before it touched the ground. She pivoted, then pointed her other hand at Rick as the old soldier chopped her head down the middle. Another blast of grey fire annihilated his head, arms and chest along with his weapons. The same flames whooshed around the Divided Woman's body and extinguished. Nothing remained of her. Rick Burnhelt fell dead on the charred ground, his lower half smoldering.

More raindrops fell. Gath sank to his knees, dumbstruck and in shock. The heat of the blackened earth singed his shins. Thunder boomed overhead. The heavens now poured down. The mechmancer looked to Xax who remained inert on his back.

"Rick." He couldn't bring himself to behold his friend's ruined body. Tears welled in his eyes, but he did not shed them. "I wish... I wish I woulda...."

Xax made a gasping noise. "I wish I woulda too." He sat up. Large raindrops pinged against his silver chassis and steamed upon the burnt ground. "Sorry about your friend."

Gath stood to his feet. He immediately bent over with his hands on his knees. He closed his eyes, willing away the sense of vertigo. "I gotta tell his kids." He looked over to the robot. "But first I need answers from you, silver guy. What are you and what is going on?"

"I'm Xax."

"No. *What* are you?"

The robot rose to his full seven feet and looked down on the mechmancer. "Gath, right?"

The shorter man nodded.

"Well, Gath. I'm the same thing as Eavae. A Weird One. And a bunch of my people want to change this world and move in. It's part of the Game they play. I don't want that. I want them stopped. And I'm gonna do the stoppin'." He extended his open metal hand. "Wanna help?"

Gath stared at the metal hand, then looked up to his jagged visor. "Eavae isn't dead, is she?"

"Nope."

Gath clasped Xax's bigger grip, unable to get the image of Rick Burnhelt's body out of his mind. "Then hell yes."

CHAPTER 2

25 Centuries Later:
The Morning of Pyrene 7th, Year Zero

Gath leaned a hand against the window. His reflection looked as terrible as he felt, so at least things were consistent. His eyes were crazed-looking and bloodshot. Sweat trickled down the sides of his forehead. And worst of all, his normally well-groomed beard looked ruffled and unkempt. He hadn't trimmed it in weeks. Not enough time for that. Not enough time for anything.

He glanced around the emptied lobby of the Kralla Hotel. Once one of the most lavish establishments in Zandris. Now vacant, with only the red-hued marble floors suggesting that this place was once something special. Serving as a forward base for the Grellish armed forces, though only two others currently occupied it with Gath. Everyone else was outside behind the blocky barricades, ready with rifles, cannons, and rocket launchers. The Krians were coming, tens of thousands of them.

Gunfire sounded in the distance. The fighting drew closer. The world was breaking. Breaking everywhere. Gath saved it once. Long ago. Well, more like Ben and Corsis saved it, and he was there to watch it with the others. Gath looked over to his silver friend. Others like Xax.

The Weird One crossed his arms with his head down. His zigzagging visor leveled at the corner where the tiled floor met the wall. He said nothing. Gath knew things were beyond bad when Xax clammed up.

The room's other occupant took a long swig from a bottle of water. His hair was shorter than usual. He had cut it a few weeks ago after some of it got burned in a battle against the Krians. A pair of scars crisscrossed over his left eye, but it was still intact. Grey, formfitting armor covered the rest of his body. Ben Burnhelt set the bottle on the bar. He ambled over to the window next to Gath.

Ben regarded Ardous Street, one of Zandris's many avenues in the hub of its government. At the barricades, Gath made note that the anxious soldiers brandished Parlestine Mark 90 rifles of his own design. That was good. High-powered and accurate. They would need them against the Krians. The dozen bulky grey suits of power armor of Ben's son's design would help as well. One soldier took a single shot at something distant. Nothing returned fire. Must have been a scout, or the soldier's nerves got the better of him.

"We were all there during the Weird War," Ben said. "All the bloodshed. I lost every family member. Veloc." Ben bit his lip for a moment. "Selene."

Gath decided to help his friend. Saying their names pained him sometimes. Ben already uttered his siblings' names. Gath spoke the names of his parents. "Rick. Cora."

Ben nodded. "I'm glad you were with my father when Eavae killed him." He tilted his head. "I wasn't there for my mother's death before that either. My father killed her during the Demon attack on Zandris. Driven mad. Or brain hacked. She wanted to kill me, then eat part of me. For Eavae's delight."

"Yeah." Gath swallowed. "That's how the story goes."

"And it keeps going. Gathering the Army of Armies. Defeating Garibald's forces. Storming the breach in Outer Yeom. We nearly lost. But we didn't. Corsis figured out a way. He made Mekem weak through Eavae. And we smote the King Weird One down." Ben closed his eyes and visibly shuddered. Gath couldn't blame him. That last fight was rough. Really rough.

Ben opened his eyes after regaining his composure. "Those nearest to his severed, disintegrating body parts became gods. Like you, Gathiner. Those farther away from the fumes became Long Lived. Like Corsis and me. We triumphed." Ben looked down at the shorter man. "That was two and a half millennia ago. It was the worst time I ever lived through."

Gath drummed his fingers on the glass of the lobby's window. The percussions echoed faintly through the mostly empty room. "Until now."

Ben nodded. "Yes." He looked over his shoulder at Xax. "I wanted to talk to the two of you before we part ways. You two never mince words." He turned his attention back to Gath. "You two tell hard truths. I need you to answer me with naked and cruel honesty. Would we be here if I had sought out Corsis after he left on his quest to cure what Mekem did to him? Helped him?"

"We wouldn't." Xax straightened up and uncrossed his arms. "We'd be worse off, Ben. He wanted to kill you. And he would have done it if you went anywhere near him. He blamed you for what Selene did. Then you and Tia hooked up. He wanted her because you got a happy ending, and he didn't. You know it. And this still would have happened. But we wouldn't have you. We wouldn't have Vick."

"But Tia might have lived."

Gath patted Ben's shoulder. "You aren't responsible for Corsis. None of us knew what he was doing. Reviving the Weird Ones' Game, making it his own. Imprisoning all of them but Xax. Using their power. Hiding in the shadows. Ruining the world. It's on him."

"He was our friend." Ben shook his head. Anguish crossed his stoic face. His ice-blue eyes creased. His brow bunched up. "I have to remind myself of that sometimes. He was going to marry Selene. He would have been family. I joked with him. He joked with me. We both pissed off Veloc."

Ben rubbed a welling tear from the edge of his eye with the heel of his hand. He looked down at Gath. "You and he developed new mechmancy disciplines." He gestured to Xax. "You saved his life against Garibald."

"I did. And I'd do it again. Because he was the only one smart enough to hamstring Mekem." Xax stepped closer to their anguished friend. "That's in the past now. You gotta stop doin' this to yourself. We need you here and now. We need Benefactor."

Ben snorted out a laugh. "Mol's joke. My fake royal title. Never going away, is it?"

"Nah. It's not." Xax shared a quick glance with Gath, who just grinned.

"Worse things to be called," the mechmancer said.

"Like God of Invention?" Ben asked.

Gath shook his head and scoffed. "Don't get me started on that stupid shit. We aren't gods. We got vast hyper powers from breathing in Mekem's disintegrating body. That's it."

Ben raised an eyebrow. "You all moved to a pico realm that you called the Heavens. Angels served you. You got more powerful as more people followed you."

Gath ran his hand down his gnarled beard. He really needed to trim it. "Okay, that is kinda god-esque when you say it like that."

Ben and Gath both laughed, the latter boisterous, the former less so. Xax didn't join them.

Gath straightened up after the moment of merriment evaporated. "Anything else anyone wants to say?"

"Yeah," Xax said. "We got our shit to do. Vurg and Muné helping the Zivonians. Ben in Haven Isle with Vick. Me at Temple Tavomine with Dave. Gath here in Zandris with Mol, Stephan, and Nis." The Weird One walked over to the window. More of the soldiers at the barricade started taking single shots at something down the street, not sustained fire. That would come soon enough.

Xax tapped his metal finger on the glass. "But first we're getting out there, and we're tearing the asses off whoever and whatever those guys are shooting at. Because...." He clenched his fist with a metallic creak.

"Because it might be the last time we see each other," Gath said. "So let's help the folks out there who need it. Do some good. Hold the line."

Xax pointed at him. "That is why I love this guy. Always has the words when you don't."

Ben gave Gath a crooked grin. "He does."

The soldiers now laid down a continuous barrage of rifle fire. Their faces ranged from tense to panicked.

Gath pulled out his modified om pistol and gestured to the door. "Words aren't always enough. After you."

PART II: XAX

CHAPTER 3

Fifteen Centuries Later:
The Morning of Pyrene 7th, 1495

Xax looked down at the trickling stream. Anniversary of the Eruption. Always a downer. Always thought of the friends lost in that awful mess. David Krullin. Bitten in half by Starm. Muné. Stabbed through the heart by Balpors. Mol and Stephan Granz. Valanis. Gathiner. All incinerated along with millions of others by the Eruption in Grelland.

The Weird One kicked a misshapen, rough-edged pebble into the flowing water. It was light enough that the current swept it away to parts unknown. Or at least parts Xax didn't care to explore. Somewhat similar to other aspects of his past.

Xax was glad Ben and Vick survived the Eruption. They saved everyone on Haven Isle. Xax and the Burnhelts reconnected about two centuries back. It wasn't like it was before. They didn't have a massive falling out. He and the family drifted apart as circular arguments never resolved. Disagreeing on how to move forward with the Holy Alliance's iron grip on the east. Disagreeing on how to go after Corsis. He and the Burnhelt's were effectively strangers to each other. It had been something like five decades since the last time he saw them, and that was just for a minute or two. Maybe he should reach out to them. Just to talk.

"What's eating you?" a deep voice asked from his side.

Xax turned to its source. Vance Vulcan popped a cashew into his mouth and munched on it. A cloth bag containing more of the nuts dangled from his meaty hand. His dark-brown skin glistened with water, soaking his closely trimmed hair and beard. He must have splashed some of the stream on his face.

His black helm was tucked under one of his thick arms. His bronze scale mail armor shimmered in the daylight.

Xax tilted his head one way, then the other. "Nothin'. Just gathering wool."

Vance swallowed the crunched up cashew. He looked around the meadow's grass rustling in the breeze, and the swaying branches and leaves of the forest beyond it. Giant puffy white clouds half-filled the sky. The Titan spread out his arms, stretching his back, before lowering them. "Never understood that expression."

"Yeah, me neither. Memorable sheep, maybe." He looked over his shoulder at the grey canvas tent in their campsite. It flapped with a gust of wind. "Marilyn and Joe still at it?"

Vance shook his head. "Just Joe grabbing some zees. Marilyn flew off about an hour ago. Said something about hunting down an Ulli that had been tailing us for the last half day."

"Coulda taken one of us with her."

Vance popped another cashew and clenched it between his teeth, speaking around it. "I think she and Joe had one of their passive-aggressive spats. She had a mean glint in her eye. Didn't want to get in her way."

"Ya' don't say." Xax stared at the tent flap. Something felt off.

Vance crunched the nut and swallowed it. He popped in two more, chewing slowly. His eyes narrowed, first gazing at the tent, then to the forest surrounding the meadow. His body language remained calm, but his deep voice spoke with muted concern. "Something's up. Talk to me."

"Gimme a sec." Xax really didn't enjoy using his extra senses to invade his friends' privacy, but something bugged him. He heard two different sets of lungs in that tent. He looked in the X-Ray wavelength, passing through the cloth and revealing Joe's skeleton, chest rising and lowering in sleep. Just Joe. No one else. But that breathing from earlier. It was gone now.

Xax turned his head to the side. He caught a glance of something billowing. Something red.

"Fuck!" He knew who was there. Xax charged into the tent. Joe didn't awaken from the sudden entry. He remained in his nylon sleeping bag. Xax's square-shaped blaster popped up from the top of his wrist. A hissing white beam fired at the seemingly vacant air above Joe. The diluted Irreality hit something, sending it careening through the fabric at the rear of the tent into the meadow.

A woman skidded along the grass, coming to a stop ten feet away. She rose slowly, not injured, not hurried. A red gown clung to her, not a thread of it burnt. A diaphanous veil obscured her face.

Joe sprang up from the sleeping bag. Now fully alert. His black hair was unkempt. He wore only underwear. The rest of his black leather armor and many weapons lay next to his sleeping bag. He pointed at the woman. He narrowed his almond-shaped eyes. His soft, raspy voice was firm but devoid of anger. "Crimsa. Undo it."

The woman in red shook her head. "Too late for that, Jovel Wrenrot."

Vance rushed next to them. "Plan?"

Joe crouched down and picked up his silver klavensol and tomauk throwing axe. "Advance. Surround. Capture."

Crimsa held out a clasped hand. A stygian-black spear materialized in her grasp. She sneered at them through the veil. "You little boys keep kicking hornets' nests. And you're mad that you finally got stung."

"You implanted your offspring in my mind." Joe's raspy voice maintained the same calmness it always did. His face looked tense, every feature tightened. It carried no fury. He spoke his next words just as evenly, though something jagged edged them. "Remove it."

Crimsa took a step forward, her gown brushing over the tall grass. "Never. You deserve every nightmare." She beckoned to them with a hooked finger. "Come closer, little ones. See how you fare."

They didn't dare do that. She would siphon their strength if Vance and Joe got any closer. Xax wasn't as vulnerable, but she had other nasty tricks that could hurt him. Charging in alone wasn't the right call here.

Joe just nodded. Xax's soft-spoken friend wasn't big on emotions. Actions were another story. The throwing axe launched at her with a swing of his arm. It twirled into the parrying haft of her spear. Fire ignited upon it, climbing up to her hands. She dropped the pole arm. It dissipated halfway to the ground. The fire remained another moment before it too extinguished. The throwing axe twirled back into Joe's grasp.

Vance threw one of his dense grenades with the speed of a rifle shot as Xax blasted another white-hot ray. Crimsa juked to the side. The spherical grenade shrieked past her head and plowed through several dozen trees in the forest directly behind her. Xax's white beam hissed past her shoulder and cored through a few more trees.

The dark spear rematerialized back into her hand. She threw it at Vance. Before he could react, Joe flung his throwing axe at it, knocking it away. Again, it returned to his hand.

She sprinted at them with the spear back leveled at them.

A new combatant swooped down on her from above and tackled Crimsa to the ground. Marilyn. Her honey-blonde flowing hair lashed in the wind. She wore gold and red chromium armor. Her feathered wings whooshed. She stabbed a bronze baslak sword alight with white holy fire upon Crimsa's back. It didn't pierce her skin or singe her gown.

Crimsa locked eyes with Joe again. Neither spoke. They didn't need to.

The woman in red sank into Marilyn's shadow like it was water just as the Angel slashed her sword to behead her.

All four of them looked at Marilyn's shadow, waiting for Crimsa to spring out of it again. A long minute passed. Their adversary did not return.

The fire on Marilyn's sword extinguished and she sheathed it at her back. She dashed toward Joe and embraced him in a fierce hug. "What happened?"

"Crimsa," Joe said, holding her just as tightly. His fingers tensed upon her armored back. His brown eyes remained fixed on the spot where Crimsa had sunk into the shadow. Still just grass ruffling in the breeze, distant leaves in the forest rustling. His face grim. "Think she was stalking us. Waiting for the right moment. She implanted a Draqu larva in my mind. Innervated me with her siphoning powers. I was out cold." He looked over to Xax. "I think she was going to plant more than one, but the loudmouth noticed her."

Marilyn pulled away from Joe. The horror painted on her face matched the roiling sensation in Xax's Irreal innards. A parasite had infected his friend. Something that would stalk his nightmares, feeding off his anguish, until it matured and took physical form when he looked into any reflective surface. The Angel shook her head. "No. Baby. No."

He placed a hand against her cheek. His tense features loosened a fraction. "It's done. Now, we need to deal with it."

Xax looked at his fingers, extending five of them one-at-a-time as he recalled the gestation period with another friend. "We've got something like five bi-months, maybe a full year before you gotta start worrying about the full grown Draqu popping out of mirrors, Joe. That's how long it took with Ben when Corsis infected him with the larva that became Crimsa."

"Benefactor." Joe glanced to Xax while squeezing Marilyn's hand. "You don't talk about him much. But he was a close friend of yours."

Xax lowered his head. "Yeah. Way back when."

"I need to talk to him. Get an idea of what to expect." Xax nodded. The tent behind them made a flapping noise with another gust. "Yeah. You do."

Marilyn bit her lip.

"What is it?" Joe asked.

"It's the Ulli, isn't it?" Vance rubbed the back of his knuckles. "Something bad."

Marilyn brushed back a strand of hair. "I caught him. Looked into his eyes. Into his vile soul. He's working for an Arch Demon in the Shade Lands. A woman in red armor. She's marshalling forces to seek a partnership with Starm's empire."

"How many are with her?" Vance asked.

"A few hundred. They will grow like weeds if we don't act."

Xax crossed his arms. They were the only ones who could act quickly enough to wreck this Arch Demon's plans. But his friend was wrecked worse. "Joe. We don't have to charge into this one. Not after what just happened. We need to get you a psionist. You're gonna have nightmares. Bad ones that will screw with your head."

Marilyn placed her hands on Joe's cheeks, her hazel eyes locked on his. "The loudmouth isn't wrong. But I'm not either. If we don't take care of this Arch Demon now. It'll take nation-states to stop her."

Joe kissed her palm, then took her hands in his. "We vote on it. Get me a psionist first. Or go after the Arch Demon first. I vote Arch Demon."

"It must be the Arch Demon," Marilyn said. "We'll get you help afterwards, baby. We will."

Joe squeezed her hand, saying nothing.

"Arch Demon," Vance said. "We have to."

They all looked at Xax. He lowered his arms. "Yer right. Yeah. All in with the Arch Demon."

Marilyn gave the Weird One an affectionate nod before she turned back to Joe. Her resolute face dissolved into one marred with guilt. "I'm so sorry, baby. I should have been here. What I said...." She trailed off, unable to finish.

"Is in the past." Joe closed his eyes and smelled her hair. Xax always found that to be one of the most endearing gestures Human couples did. The swordsman whispered, "Let's keep it there."

CHAPTER 4

Four Weeks Later:
The Afternoon of Pyrene 38th, 1495

Wind howled atop the Outer Wall, passing between the six people gathered atop it. Low-hanging clouds on one side, a hellish inferno on the other. It towered taller than most buildings at three-thousand feet. The air was thin, though not chilled. The heat from the unnatural fire it contained made heat mirages across its entire width of five-hundred-feet. It showed no signs of erosion despite its millennia and a half age. Its tan-brown stone had been erected by Vurg's vast etherea and Gathiner's machines.

Gath. Xax couldn't believe it. His old friend wasn't dead. That was one of many items of discussion with the two men in front of him, Ben and Vick Burnhelt.

Ben wore his long hair in a ponytail at his back. He wore grey and blue chromium armor with a Grellish Claw over his heart. His face looked harder than the last time Xax had seen him a century ago.

Vick's face was covered by his helmet. His purple eyes were visible through transparent metal eye holes, one of them appearing slightly enlarged because of the monocle lens over it. A piecemeal selection of gadgets covered the rest of his white power armor, including a few clockwork devices that ticked on his chest.

Joe, Marilyn, and Vance stood behind Xax, saying nothing, just as he had asked them.

Ben finally broke the silence after the latest fierce gust died down. "Why here, Xax? We could have done this in Ruby."

Xax scraped one of his feet upon the wall's stone. "'Cuz it's harder for Corsis to eavesdrop on us here. It's harder for me to use my extra senses, at least."

Ben just snorted at that. "But not impossible."

Xax made a blowing-out-a-sigh noise. He didn't breathe, but he sometimes liked making that Human non-verbal response. Of course, he added something verbal because he was all about saying stuff. "Nah."

Ben and Xax both stayed quiet following that. Xax knew Ben came to the same conclusion. If Corsis wanted to spy on them, he would find a way to do it. Even here.

"Good to see you again," Vick said. His helmet modulated his voice with an electric echo. "For what it's worth."

Xax just pointed at the mechmancer with an affectionate tilt of his head. Vick's failed attempt to change the subject and disarm the tension reminded Xax of why he always liked the kid. Kid. That term no longer applied. Vick crept up on his three-thousandth birthday in a handful of decades.

"Yeah." Xax looked at the white light of the daystar, shining high in the sky. He brought his gaze back down to the pair of Grells. "Ok, let's get to it. We... we need some help." He jutted a thumb over his shoulder at Joe. His friend wore his black leather armor that included a cowl that covered all of his face except for his almond-shaped eyes and the upper bridge of his nose. "Crimsa did the same thing to him Corsis did to you, Ben. Implanted a Draqu larva in his mind."

"Fuck," Vick said. His arm trembled with a clenched fist. His other hand joined it, now visibly quaking. "FUCK!"

"You should have led with that." Ben strode past Xax toward Joe, scrutinizing him with eyes faintly glowing. The wind ruffled Ben's hair as he did it. "Vick, can you think straight right now?"

Vick didn't answer immediately. His heaving breaths steadied over the next few seconds, still amplified by his helmet's speakers. A quartet of holographic 2-D screens then flickered in front of Vick, and he pressed a series of commands on his virtual displays. "Yeah, Dad. I'm on it."

"Mmm," Ben murmured, his pale, faintly illuminated eyes still locked on Joe's face.

Joe looked right back at Ben, neutral and steady.

While both Burnhelt's made their analyses in silence, Xax paced off to the side. He beckoned with a curled finger to Marilyn and Vance. The Angel and Titan joined him. "Maril knows this from her time hanging with Vurg, but this might be news to you, Vance. Vick's mom was killed by Crimsa. She died protecting him from her. He was just a baby at the time."

Marilyn glanced over to Vick with a pensive expression. She scrutinized him, no doubt making use of her Angelic empathic vision, searching for any overt emotions radiating from the mechmancer.

Vance leaned in closer and spoke with muted tones, which were no doubt lost in the breezy air. "And Benefactor didn't even blink when you told him about Crimsa. This guy is stone cold, Xaxy."

"Kinda," Xax said, thinking back to those bad days right after Corsis made the Game his own. "Ben was a wreck for a good long time after Tia died. But he's good at pushing things aside 'til later. Only gotten better as time goes on. Vick is a little more of a heart-on-his-sleeve kinda guy."

Vance scratched the side of his well-trimmed beard. "And here I thought we were on the top of Crimsa's shit list after the stuff we did."

Xax shook his head. "Ben and Vick are right there with us. Right there."

Marilyn kept her gaze on the armored mechmancer. Her expression softened. "He carries a lot of weight on his shoulders."

Xax lowered his head, remembering a lot of dead friends, a lot of guilt. "Plenty of that goin' around."

Another couple of minutes passed before Vick's holograms flickered away. "No sign of it."

"She's there," Joe said with his eyes still fixed on those of Ben. "She's already introduced herself to me. Calls herself Mary Night."

"I believe you," Vick said. "I just can't verify it."

Ben chose that moment to look away from Joe. He massaged his temples. His eyes ceased their faint glow. "Nor can I."

Joe kept his calm brown eyes on Ben. "So what can I do?"

"I can only give you suggestions on how to cope. How to deny her." Ben crossed his forefinger over the crisscrossed scar over his left eye. "But she will hurt you. And she will break free. She will. And then she will hurt others."

Marilyn covered her mouth and looked up at Xax, silently asking him to deny Ben's prediction.

Xax placed a hand on her shoulder and just nodded to confirm the truth.

She folded her wings tightly against her back as Xax pulled his hand away, her face tight.

Joe's shoulders tensed, which was his version of throwing a hissy fit. "That's... not at all ideal."

"It is not, Arms Master." He gestured to the blazing expanse of the Fire Well. "We cannot destroy her as my homeland was. But you can mitigate her influence on your mind. Study concepts that bend thoughts. Riddles. Jokes. Puzzles. Mazes. Visualize them. Put them between you and her. They are your armor. Your buffer."

Joe crossed his arms. "Noted."

"She will find you sometimes. When she does, ask her questions without answers. Get her talking rather than attacking."

Ben then gestured to the low-hanging clouds on the outside of the Fire Well. "She will one day manifest in physical reality when you look at your reflection. Avoid it as long as possible, but you won't be able to avoid it forever. At some point, you will look at something shiny, something that glimmers." Ben set his jaw before continuing, no doubt remembering when Crimsa first manifested. "And she will appear. Kill her if you can. Her kind are weakest when they first gain flesh."

"Is there anything we can do before that?" Marilyn asked. "My holy fire burns ghosts and spectral matter. Is there some way to dive into his mind? Burn her out?"

"Not without knowing where she is. You would just harm or kill Jovel Wrenrot."

"And what about that last option?" Joe asked, his soft voice just as flat as always.

"No!" Marilyn yelled. "I won't allow it."

Ben gestured to the Angel with an out-swept hand. "Agreed. Not an option."

"Why?"

Ben's face hardened. "Because you are the Arms Master. Vurg's warrior without peer. You don't get to give up. You have the combined experience of David Krullin and my wife. They did not die so you could avoid a hard road."

"And I now know you value my life. Greatly. Good to know."

Xax had to hand it to Joe. He knew how to get people to say what they felt.

The swordsman tapped the side of his cowled head. "I'll keep her here forever. She will not escape."

Ben gave him a wan smile. "I hope you're right. Prepare as if she will break free."

Joe nodded. His shoulders loosened, though his stance remained rigid, ready for trouble.

Another gust cut into them, rippling Marilyn's hair and wing feathers, making Ben's hair lash again. When it abated, Xax girded himself. He needed to get the other thing out now. Joe had some answers. Ben and Vick needed the news. "So. There's something you said earlier. You were wrong."

"Out with it, Xax," Ben said.

"The Fire Well didn't incinerate your homeland. It survived. Got moved somewhere else."

Ben stared at the Weird One for an uncomfortably long stretch of breaths. "That is a very terrible joke, old friend."

Vick stepped next to his father. "You're serious."

"Yeah. I am. We just made a trip into the Shade Lands. Went after someone we *thought* was an Arch Demon. She was putting together an army to attack you guys. We got her to stop. Snapped her out of a bad head space."

Ben's brow creased in an intense frown.

"It's Mol. She's wearing the ViRauni armor."

Vick leaned closer. "Mol Granz. The Queen of Old Grelland. *That* Mol?"

"Yep."

Vick pointed at Joe. "His predecessor and I killed the last one to wear that armor."

Xax nodded. "You and Dave Krullin. Team supreme. Took her down. I actually thought it was Jarah in the armor until she took off the helmet."

"How is she alive?" Ben asked. "How is Old Grelland... Grelland still intact?"

"Gath's machine didn't fail in the Eruption. He had a plan B that he engineered on the fly. Shunted everything to a pico realm called Pendulum. Saved everyone. From the fire. Not from what came afterwards. Dread Corps set up shop there. They used fleshmancy and these plants to mind hack people. Transform them into soldiers for Dread Corps."

Vick and Ben shared a glance.

"What?"

"Keep going," Vick said. "We'll tell you when you're done."

Xax shrugged. He'd hold them to that. As usual, the Burnhelt's knew something about something. They were good at that. "Dread Corps and their converts overran Transvahlu, took it over. Turned it into their forward base. They invaded Kytine and Setu Sene, pushed their way to Zandris. Our side stood against them. Stephan died. It got desperate. Mol put on the ViRauni armor. She turned the tide with Gath and Nis. It ended in a stalemate. Dread Corps on the west side of the Mirror Sea. The remains of Grelland on the east side."

"And Mol went mad," Vick said. "It did the same thing to Jarah."

"Turns out there's a twist," Xax said. "It only does that if the one wearing it steps foot in any part of Grelland. New or Old. She fled. And lost herself." He held up a clenched fist and ignited his glowing cone, covering it. "A punch with this snapped her out of it."

Ben nodded. "Your diluted Irreality. Always unpredictable with its effects."

Xax turned off the cone. "That's the idea."

Vick looked around with a slow turn of his neck, no doubt searching for signs of Mol in hiding atop the otherwise desolate top of the wall. "So where is she?"

"She helped us kill or scatter the army she put together. When that was done, she walked off. Tried to stop her. She said she'd fight us to the death if we didn't back off. We believed her. So we let her go. Don't know where she went."

"Did she say how she got from the pico realm to the Shade Lands?" Ben gazed at the azure, smokeless blaze that stretched to the horizon. "We'll never find a way to Grelland if we don't have directions."

"I asked. Mol couldn't remember. She didn't have her head on straight. She'd lost decades of memories. Centuries maybe. I've been there. After the Eruption. Whole lotta shit I did, I can't remember. She's in the same boat."

"Unfortunate."

"Sucktacular is what it is, Ben. We know Gath, Nis, and probably millions of others are still alive. Fighting Dread Corps to survive. And we can't get to them. Sucktacular is definitely the word."

Xax's old friend gave him a sedate, lopsided grin.

"This changes a lot." Vick placed both hands on the back of his helmet with his elbows spread out. "Holy fuck. Just holy fuck. Grelland. Mol. Aunt Nis. Gath."

Xax chuckled without mirth. "Yeah. Kinda terrible. Kinda not." He made a beckoning motion with his hand. "I told you my stuff. Now you gotta tell me what that looky-loo that you two gave each other was about."

Ben exhaled a long breath through his nose. "Those plants are called Kliosts. Hekati had a hand in creating them. She's got them pollinating airborne spore that brain hacks in large enough doses. It's limited to Stretch right now, but spreading by the day. We're scrambling to contain it. I'm guessing Hekati helped Corsis in adapting them in this Pendulum realm."

"I'm working on something to neutralize the spore." Vick made a pinching motion with his thumb and forefinger. "Nanobots."

Xax gave the mechmancer an affirming nod. Good to know Vick was as sharp as ever, probably sharper.

Ben gestured to the western horizon. "Do you want to visit New Grelland? Get some rest someplace where you don't have to look over your back. The Sibyls might have more insight into Mr. Wrenrot's infection as well."

Xax scuffed his metal foot along the stone beneath him again. "We've both changed. We don't see eye to eye on much anymore. It won't be like it was before, Ben."

"I know that. But it can be like it is now. A group of people on the same side who work together on occasion."

Xax looked over to Joe, Marilyn, and Vance. Marilyn spoke for them. "We go with them. They might be able to help Joe. End of discussion."

That was reason enough right there. Xax turned back to the Grells. "Take us on the tour, Benefactor."

Ben just gave him another crooked grin. Even though everyone called him by that title as a sign of respect, Xax knew he still thought of it as an inside joke. A jest given to him by another friend who chose to stay lost.

PART III: JOVEL WRENROT

CHAPTER 5

One Year Later:
The Late Morning of Blite 40th, 1496

Joe sprinted upon a walkway atop a giant plastic pipe used for tube trains. His shadow stretched out before him in the cloudless afternoon sky. Lush rainforests surrounded him for fifty feet before giving way to a parched desert. The Mad Lands always disoriented him whenever he ventured here. The topography radically shifted every few trecs because of the etherea spewed out by the Fire Well, which bordered them.

He held Poison in one hand and three Fangs between the fingers of the other. A pair of Alliance Knights holding spiked maces rushed in front of him. A trio of Fethelithers pressed on him from behind, clashing their scythed hands together.

The Arms Master pivoted and threw the three daggers in his hand at the shadowy Demons. They left his hand as though fired from a gun. The three Fangs punched through their chests and out their backs. They evaporated into black mist as the throwing knives rematerialized in his bandolier. Joe turned again, pulling Stained from a sheath at his back.

"*I'm coming out, Joey*," Mary whispered in his head. "*Can't stop me.*"

"*Fuck*," he thought. She was in his waking mind now, no longer his nightmares. Just as the Grellish Sibyls warned. No time. No time. He was in a fight. Worry about it later.

The two Alliance Knights reached him and swung their maces at him simultaneously. Stained deflected one mace while Joe stabbed Poison through the other Knight's shoulder and then evaded the mace by sinking on split legs. The Arms Master jumped to his feet and back-flipped away from the other Knight as his partner fell limp to the flat surface of the tube's walkway.

"*Oh, we can fuck if that's what you want,*" Mary whispered. The hair on the back of Joe's neck stood up. She wasn't real, but he felt her breath on his ear. "*But you always put things between us. I could give you delights that the Angel can't. Just let me out. Freely.*"

Joe couldn't let her distract him. In a fight. In a fight. Focus. He parried the Allied soldier's next strike, then the next, and the next. Good. Rhythm. Keep it up.

"*You know it's inevitable, Joey,*" Mary said, her immaterial breath cold in his ear. "*It's why you snuck away from your friends last night. Chasing down the Horrinshal based on sketchy rumors. These poor idiots might have just been on reconnaissance. You could have let them pass without a problem.*"

A pair of disembodied hands materialized next to him. They glowed white. There was a mancer nearby. Wrenrot leapt off the tube as electric bolts struck the spot where he had stood. He landed on a sandy dune in a tumbling roll and stood up with Stained replaced by two more Fangs that he threw at the hands without a body. They rifled in the air, spiraling like bullets rather than twirling like throwing daggers. The Fangs tore through the hands' palms. They bled grey ectoplasm and slowly faded from view.

"*But you can't ever let things lie,*" she hissed with sadistic glee. "*Always have to step in. It's why my mother infected you with me. She wanted to fuck you up. You deserved it.*"

Ignore it. Have to keep moving. Joe took off running again, huffing with every step. He pulled three more Fangs from the bandolier. A new trio of blades grew from the bandoleer's once empty spots. A lake loomed ahead as the desert made an abrupt transition to grasslands on the far side. A spiky tentacle lunged out of the lake and snaked towards Joe. This had to be the mancer. Maybe a Krakenite, or something else. He couldn't tell.

"*So, do you feel good and fucked yet, Joey?*"

The Fangs streaked from the swordsman's hands and bounced off the crusted hide of the spiky tentacle. Joe lunged to the ground when the tentacle lashed at his head. He unsheathed Phantom with his free hand and turned over on his back. The klavensol stabbed through the tentacle's bony, slime-covered hide followed by another stab of Poison in the same spot. The tentacle reeled away from him halfway back to the lake before limply collapsing on the sand and jagged rocks along the lakeshore. Poison's oily venom was supposed to kill it, but he had to be sure.

The swordsman wearily approached the lake in a jog, leaving footprints behind in the tan sand. He replaced Poison with Stained to compliment Phantom. When Wrenrot reached the rocky shore of the lake, green mucus bubbled from its center. It smelled of rot, of death. The swordsman stood silently over the lake, awaiting more attackers. None came. He'd slain the entire Horrinshal cell.

He shuddered and lowered his head with his eyes closed. Focus. Keep her trapped. Think of a riddle. Keep her turning corners. No straight-a-ways. "I have fingers, but no toes," he said aloud. "What am I?"

"*Pathetic,*" he thought. "*So tired. Can't come up with anything better. She'll get this immediately. She'll turn the corner and slash my throat.*"

To his surprise, Mary ceased her taunts.

He slowed his panting from his exertion, trying to calm himself. But he had to keep moving. Don't let her creep in the edges.

Joe opened his eyes. Beholding the untainted water near his feet. And his reflection within it. The form of a woman instantly materialized within the water's shiny surface. "Shit!"

Joe pivoted just as Mary Night's body materialized behind him, taking on matter and color upon a small dune. Her olive skin glistened with moisture, as though she had actually emerged from the lake. Her long purple hair was also soaked and swept behind her. Deep-violet serpent glyph tattoos twined down the sides of her neck, twisting behind to her back. She wore black, formfitting leather with fishnets stretching between her ample breasts down to her navel. Mary held bladed weapons ready, a grand stiletto and a filv. Her eyes, black with purple irises, fumed with a madness.

"I'm here." She gave him a soft smile. One of affection. "And the riddle's answer is gloves. Pretty easy."

"Yes." Joe's swords remained lowered. As did hers. Benefactor told him to kill her as soon as she emerged. Grant no mercy. That would come in time. If this didn't work. "Mary. Can you stop?"

She raised an eyebrow. "Stop what?"

"The horrors that you performed in my mind. Can you stop from reenacting them out here? In my waking world?"

Mary remained still. The edges of her lips quivering. Repressing a laugh or a scream, he couldn't tell.

He pressed on with his point. "You didn't have a choice before. I understand that. Your mother implanted you in my mind. Compelled to torment me to grow, to gain strength. You couldn't stop yourself on the inside. You had to mature into an adult. Now that you're on the outside, it's your choice. Possibilities lie before you." A tear ebbed from the side of Joe's eye. He didn't want to fight her. She was a lost soul. He had to help her. If she would allow it. "Ones that don't involve bringing my nightmares, *our* nightmares, to life."

"Your voice is so much softer out here. Frail. Whispery. Damaged." A tear also rolled down her cheek. It glistened in the daylight with the rest of the moisture covering her. "How did you hide this from me? This plea? I should have known about it."

"You didn't find out everything about me." He swallowed dryness to the back of his throat. "But that's beside the point. I want you to know that I don't hate you. I don't want you to feel like we have to go down the road in front of us. We can step off of it."

"Joey. Oh, Joey." Her face lit up with mania. She took a step forward on her high-heeled boots with a dull thunk in the soft, grassy earth. Her trembling lips let out the melodic and unhinged cackle that had haunted his dreams for greater than a year. "I want this so bad I *can't stand it.*"

The Arms Master did not hesitate. The plea had failed. Now she had to die. His swords slashed at her throat before she could stab her grand stiletto at *his* throat, as he knew she would. She parried both of his swords with her filv and back-flipped away from him.

She backed away from him, pointing both blades at him, stirring up the sand as she did it. He pressed forward with her retreat. Her smile lessened. "Am I everything you dreamed I would be? Everything you wanted?"

"Yes." Joe replaced Stained with three Fangs. They streaked at her like bullets. Mary sidestepped each one.

"The world's going to bleed!" The Draqu bolted away from him over the dunes. She cackled again, as though someone maliciously tickled her. "And you have to watch it."

She ran next to the giant tube along the ground's countless coarse grains. Joe threw another barrage of throwing knives. She wove through them with the grace of a ballerina. She vanished into the tube's thin shadow.

Joe stared at that spot that slowly blew away with grit in the breeze. Waiting for her, just as he had waited for her mother. Minutes and minutes passed. Mary Night did not return.

He had just unleashed a horror into the world. He came out here away from his friends because he knew they wouldn't let him talk to her. Wouldn't let him try to get her to get off the road. A road she had just gleefully run down. He had to make it right. Both to stop her and to convince her.

There was still a chance. A small one. Mary had wept as he had. He reached her. But it wasn't enough.

He stared at the same spot as the shadow grew longer with the ebbing of the daystar in the sky. More minutes elapsed. Maybe an hour. He did not know. The sounds of insects and larger fauna grew louder all around him. The day was ending. Worse things would soon stalk him. That didn't concern him. Marilyn had already found him.

She touched down at his side with a whoosh of her white wings, sending up a few swirls of sand. The Angel didn't say anything at first. She just took his hand in hers and kissed his knuckles. "She's out, isn't she?"

Joe shifted his gaze to her soulful blue eyes. "I couldn't get through to her."

Her expression hardened a bit, but still nuanced with affection. "You should have had me with you. I would have–"

"Killed her before I could say a word." Joe pulled his hand away. "Don't pretend, Marilyn. We both know you would have."

Marilyn stepped closer to him, touching his nose against hers. Her eyes now widened with anger. "You fucking idiot. Of fucking course I would have. You screamed every night in your sleep as she chased you in your dreams. Tortured your mind. She is a gods damned parasite who deserves to burn. Vance and Xax would have done the same thing."

Joe closed his eyes. Another few tears ebbed down his cheek. "That's why I ran from all of you. I knew she was emerging. I had to try."

"Look at me," Marilyn said with a quiet voice that brooked no defiance.

Joe opened his eyes. Her expression had changed to one full of frailty, with shadows crossing her face with the encroaching dusk. "I need you to tell me you had no relations with her in your mind. Again."

Joe took her hand again, interlocking his fingers with hers. "I didn't have sex with her. I didn't kiss her. I didn't get mesmerized by her."

The Angel's skeptical expression told Joe that she remained skeptical. His lover then scowled. "Mary. Marilyn. You can't tell me she only took her name because it's a flip of nightmare. She did it to dig into your affection for me. Twist it. Make you act stupid. Like now."

Joe tightened his grip on her hand. "It wasn't because of her name. Or because of any fondness." He tightened his lips before continuing. "I wanted her to renounce her mother's mandate. I wanted her to choose anything but the road laid out before her."

Marilyn's eyebrows raised. "Why?"

Joe ground his teeth for a few moments. "Because she came from my mind. She's not my child. But my thoughts influenced her in her larval state. I had to try to reach her. I had to."

Marilyn hugged him. "You big-hearted fool. I don't need to tell you what happens now. Your guilt will do all of that."

"I know. It already is." Joe hugged her back. He was so unbelievably lucky to have this Angel in his life. Her love for him was limitless, even now when she should be berating him with his folly. So he did it for her. "I have unleashed a monster on the world. Everything she does is on me."

"We have to hunt her," Marilyn whispered in his ear, squeezing him tighter as the shadows of night pressed in on all sides. "Burn every favor. Turn every stone. And slay her."

Joe nodded. He did not say something that burned in his heart. If he could do it over again, he'd still try to break through Mary Night's madness. Maybe he could have said something different. Done something different. He would have tried anything.

That chance was now past him. She was on the road created by her mother. And he and his friends had to chase her down it.

CHAPTER 6

Two Years Later:
The Afternoon of Quatres 1st, 1498

Joe kicked through the executive suite's door. Someone on the other side toppled over at his sudden entrance. He surprised them. Good.

Blood streaked down the giant floor-to-ceiling panoramic windows, giving the environs a dark-red pallor. Twenty naked bodies drained of blood hung by their feet from the vaulted carbon-mesh ceiling. Their necks slit. Their skin ranging in color from blue to red to pitch black to alabaster white. They were Chromatics, the most common Post Human race on Trojis. No. They weren't anything but dead now.

Dead because of the crazy people in this suite and the rest of their cult. Dead because of Mary Night. Because of Jovel Wrenrot. Because of the people in front of him. They were Keepers who Mary recruited. All wearing glyph tattoos like hers. Some armed with blood-covered blades. Others with particle rifles leveled from behind toppled desks that served as barricades.

Joe thrust his klavensol into the bare chest of a blue-skinned man with blood painted in a spiraling pattern over his face. Phantom's immaterial blade passed through his flesh without actually touching it but killing him all the same. He threw Scorch into the neck of another cultist, a red-skinned woman. Her entire head ignited with a flare as the hand axe flew back to Joe's grasp.

That left another eight of Mary Night's cultists, three of them armed with particle rifles. Joe dove to the side as a barrage of azure particle beams filled with black flecks perforated the door and wall behind him. He sheathed Phantom on the way down and rolled farther to the opposite wall. He popped up to his knees and threw four Fangs and Scorch at them. His throwing knives buried into an eye of each cultist, including those armed with the energy rifles. The hand axe split the skull of another female Chromatic, then immolated her. The knives vanished and rematerialized back in their sheaths in his bandolier. Scorch again twirled back to his grasp.

The remaining three charged Joe, but they only made it two steps. A hissing white beam swept across them and cut them in half. Their severed bodies fell to the floor in a cauterized, twitching mass.

Xax crouched through the ruined doorway. "The crew on the other floor is done. Mary isn't there. Heard the party goin' up here, and figured I'd crash it."

Joe nodded to the Weird One and stood. "This is the last spot in the building. She has to be in the next room."

"Yeah, that's what I figured too."

"Marilyn and Vance?" Joe asked.

Xax pointed downward. "Still in the subbasement fighting those mechs. Mary screwed with a lot of people's heads. She knew we were coming and set off this revolt of crazies. The Keepers are going bat shit trying to contain this mess."

Xax moved closer to him. The lanky metal man moved with quiet grace. His pointed-tipped feet made zero sounds. He crouched again, bringing his metal, zigzagging visor to eye level. "Joe. I'm taking point. And you're gonna let me."

Joe clenched his jaw. Xax wasn't affected by the Draqu's life force siphoning powers. He was by far the best suited of them to face off with Mary. But he knew Xax had another reason. He thought Joe couldn't go through with killing her. Couldn't fight her. He was wrong. Joe would end her life today. He nodded. "Just let me talk to her before the end."

"Will if I can." Xax straightened up and turned toward the carnage before them.

"Xax?"

"Yeah, buddy?"

"Thanks." Joe swallowed hard. "Thanks for not rubbing my nose in this mess. My mess."

"I'm a dick sometimes. But not that big of a dick. You're already beating yourself up about it way worse than any of us could."

"I am." Everyone who suffered and died at Mary Night's hands was on him and his delusional mercy. Mercy that he would still extend if he could do it again. Each death she inflicted was a link in a chain that would drag him down into an ocean of despair. That reckoning would come later. Joe gestured to another door in the corner. "She's in the observation lounge. After you."

Xax stepped around the dead bodies dangling from the ceiling and those they had just killed. Joe followed with soft footsteps, the bloodless faces of those hanged from the ceiling imprinting themselves in his mind with all the other visages of the dead. He pushed those images away. Had to stay sharp. But those images would never leave him, and they would always creep in from the edges of his psyche. He knew this. Just as he knew that Mary Night would not escape this time. The certainty hummed in his bones.

The Weird One reached the door and gave Joe a nod. Joe nodded back. Xax kicked the door with a stomp that send it flying like cardboard in a gale. It flew inward into the observation lounge. Red light tinged these environs as well. A panoramic window ringed the interior with transparent omsteel. Blood painted every inch, not in splotchy clumps of gore, but neatly glazed. No bodies hung in this room or lay on the floor. Tables and cushioned chairs were toppled, broken, ripped, and stained.

From the encircling window, the daystar shone over the cityscape of Crystal Keep. Networked spires of metal buildings and vast urban canyons stretched to the horizon in all directions. The city-state's famed trec-tall curtain wall was too far away to be seen. Joe concerned himself with someone on a far smaller scale, but far more immense in less tangible aspects.

The woman from his bad dreams sat in the only intact chair along the window to their left. She slouched with one leg crossed over the other, her foot idly bobbing. The viscera matted her long purple hair to her head. Blood also glazed much of her form-fitting attire. Her black stiletto and her silver dagger with a long, serrated blade rested on the chair's arms on either side of her. She wore that same gleefully ecstatic expression. "Hi, boys."

"No shadow shifting this time, Mary," Xax said.

She nodded. "Yes, the Keepers and their super tech. Pains in the ass."

That was the source of Joe's certainty of Mary's inability to flee through shadows. The Keepers used an upgraded array of jammers that prevented space bending. Through the last five bloody weeks, she had used the shadows with impunity in her escalating murder spree. Their prior jammers couldn't hinder her. Their new ones just activated this morning did indeed stop her. The machines were in the bowels of this very building. Marilyn and Vance beat back her will-depleted followers from wrecking them while Xax and Joe chased her to the top of this skyscraper. To this room. With nowhere else to hide.

She gave Joe a wan stare of her black and purple eyes. "I think you were right, Joey. I tried to stop myself, just to see if I could." The edge of her lips trembled, either stifling a fit of weeping or laughter. "I couldn't." Her eyes widened, desperate and maddened. "I couldn't!"

"Shut up." Xax took a stomping step forward. "I'd ask if you want this to go easy or hard, but that's a stupid question, ain't it?"

The conflicted expression evaporated from her face. Insanity bubbled forth anew. She winked at them. "The stupidest."

Xax bolted at her and fired his wrist-mounted cable claw at her arm. She blurred to the side, dodging it, with her long knives now brandished in each hand. She howled out an unhinged cackle. "I'm super charged with super people! Super charged!"

The metal man adjusted his heading. A glowing cone flashed around his right hand when he made a fist. Mary leapt at him with her blades, aiming for his left side. Xax moved with identical super speed, parried her strike with his left cylindrical forearm, and jabbed his right energized fist into her throat. She bounced against the transparent metal window with a dull thud and a startled gasp.

Xax fired his cable claw at her wrist and coiled around it. He reeled her in again. This time, he grabbed her neck with his segmented hand as the cable and its metal claw retracted back into his left wrist. He punched her seven times in the face with the glowing cone.

Joe bit his lip. He wanted to enter the fray. Help Xax. But he couldn't. She'd enervate him if he got any closer. He had to watch. And wait.

Mary showed no signs of harm. The blood of the others evaporated from her face, but she wasn't even bruised. She dropped her stiletto and the serrated dagger. She smiled at him the entire time. "Super charged, dickless. Super charged."

"Super," Xax said in a flat deadpan.

She pressed her feet against Xax's chest and leapt from his grip. She retrieved the stiletto and serrated dagger, cackling all the while. The spree killer beckoned to him with her index finger. "I can't siphon you. But I can beat your metal ass. We both know it."

Xax bent on his knees, ready to strike. "But I got the beat, Mary. I got it good."

The Draqu pointed both blades at the Weird One. "Then dance, dickless. Dance!"

Xax balled his other hand. A cone surrounded it. He slammed them together with sparks of energy. He leapt at her with arms and legs flailing in that faux-sloppy fighting style. She blurred away, evading his lunge. Her black stiletto stabbed his head. The blade glanced off his silver finish. Xax sent a right hook into her face and knocked her against the see-through wall. "Like that move? I got others I can bust. Plenty of others."

Mary sprang at him again and stabbed his stomach with the serrated dagger. The blade also did not penetrate Xax's metallic hide. She side-stepped his double uppercut and kneed him in the teeth with an upward leap.

Joe replaced his hand axe with Stained, his red, crystalline short sword. He needed to pick his moment. Wait for her to focus her attention completely on Xax.

Xax fell on his back with her on top of him. She stabbed her daggers into his plated visor with both hands, with a loud clank. Her arms quivered as the blade pressed into his face, and a metallic shriek sounded from the increased pressure.

Joe readied Stained. He had to be absolutely sure she didn't notice him.

Mary bit her lip, eyes widened with frustration. "I'll pierce this shell, you fucking–"

Joe pointed Stained at her face and a searing red beam projected into her forehead, making a horrid sizzle. She screamed in pain. Xax slugged her with an uppercut, sending her hurtling away. He fired his claw cable at her as she flew toward the transparent wall, this time encircling both of her legs.

The Weird One leapt to his feet and reeled her back. The cable coiled around her waist, pinning her arms together, and stopping at her shoulders. Xax grabbed her by the throat. An energy cone ignited over his free hand.

He punched her once. Twice. Thrice. Snapping her head back each time. She looked dazed, but otherwise unharmed. Neither her nose nor her mouth bled.

Xax set her back on her feet and pivoted around her, clamping his metal hands on each of her shoulders. "Say what you need to say, Joe. She can't siphon ya for a minute or so."

Joe strode toward her with slow, deliberate strides. "Mary. This is where the road ends. The road I tried to get you to step away from. I shouldn't have done that."

The swordsman leveled Stained at her chest as he reached the halfway point between him and the woman of his nightmares. "I should have killed you when you emerged. I should have had Marilyn, Vance, and Xax with me. Every death. Is my fault. And yours."

She gasped in a sobbing breath. "I couldn't help myself, Joey. Can you...." Tears ebbed down the sides of her face. "Can you help me?"

Joe was three steps away from her now. "I can."

She smiled at him with serene relief. "I'm so glad. Send me away. Send me far away."

Joe plunged Stained's glassy blade into her heart, taking care not to run her through since Xax was right behind her. She gasped in agony, but she didn't writhe. She didn't fight the death she had earned. Crimson light then shone out of every orifice on her body. Joe stepped back, leaving the filv's blade buried in her chest.

She sucked in a shuddering breath. Illumination pulsated from her eyes and mouth. Her gasping changed to a low-pitched moan and then diminished to nothing. Her head drooped. Inky blood gushed from her chest and drooled from her mouth, starkly contrasting the red and purple blood of Chromatics soaking her clothes. The light of Stained no longer shone from her body.

"You can let her go, Xax." Joe pulled Stained out of her heart. He sheathed both it and Phantom.

Xax shook her once, waited another moment, and then nodded. His claw cable uncoiled from her body and withdrew into the top of his left wrist. Xax gently pushed her lifeless corpse into Joe's arms.

The swordsman shrank to his knees as her body sagged downward. He lifted her head and looked at her wide, lifeless eyes a few seconds before they and the rest of her body deteriorated into dust. Joe blinked away tears as even the dust on his hands disintegrated into nothingness. "Go far, Mary Night. Go far away."

Xax and Joe said nothing to each other. Joe couldn't raise his head.

Time passed, maybe a little, maybe more. Joe kept looking at his hands until he felt a light touch on his shoulder. He already knew it was Marilyn. He gazed up at her loving face, blurred from his weeping. "I'm finished."

She took his hand and squeezed it.

Vance ambled around her to Xax. He tried to whisper quietly, but Joe heard it anyway. "Mechs are wrecked. Her cultists weren't will hacked. She just convinced hundreds of unstable people in key positions to follow her lead. There's a lot of discontent in this city."

"And it's about ta get leveled at us," Xax said softly, but a little louder than Vance. "We gotta jet."

"We do." Marilyn tightened her grip on Joe's hand and pulled him to his feet. She gently pressed her forehead against his, her blue eyes boring into his soul. "Mary Night is finished. You are not, Jovel Wrenrot. Not fucking yet."

PART IV: HARRY MANG

CHAPTER 7

Harry Mang ran like hell in an erratic weaving pattern. Searing rays of sickly green light shrieked just to the side of his shoulder. *"Shit! Keep moving. Keep random. Keep living."* The wrecked artrak smoldered fifty feet away. He just had to make it to that. Get some cover. Pick them off.

The young Alliance Knight juked downward just before another green beam streaked where his head would have been. He nearly stumbled in the plains' thick grass, but he maintained his footing. Twenty feet. *"Keep focused. Every moment you live is a moment they aren't shooting at Diana and the others. Kill as many as you can."*

A missile roared from behind. Harry glanced, instinctively took aim with his needle gun, and took a single shot at the reinforced warhead's red paint. It exploded well behind him, the burning conflagration giving him the cover he needed to reach the charred husk of the artrak. He turned and peeked out from around the armored vehicle's chassis.

Dozens of green dots shone through the clearing fire. Each one connected to a one-eyed cyborg, a Cykot. Dread Corps's shock troops. Harry didn't wait for the smoke to clear. He breathed and shot. Breathed and shot. Again and again. Each magnetically accelerated bullet pierced their eyes. He killed at least ten of them before they started shooting back with emerald beams from their optics.

Harry took cover behind the artrak as the beams sizzled into it, glad his helmet's air supply kept the stench of ozone that accompanied the beams. He ran to the other side and picked the attackers off with the same unerring precision, eliminating more of their numbers with his standard issue rifle. Harry knew he had talent, but with every fight, he wondered just how much of his good fortune was extraordinary luck, and how much was natural ability.

He couldn't get overconfident. Dread Corps never let him. No matter how many he killed, more always emerged to fill their ranks. Usually something worse. Case in point. A building-sized Titanborg stomped toward him, with the remaining Cykots following behind it. The infantry used the black armor plating of the metal giant's massive humanoid body as cover. It was the source of the missile that Harry had shot down. This foe had no weak points to exploit.

But that didn't mean that it had no weaknesses. Harry timed his shots with the movements of the Titanborg's legs. He fired at another Cykot's centrally positioned eye, killing the foe instantly. This set off a frenzy. The remaining Cykots fired a barrage of green rays and the Titanborg let loose with a pair of high-caliber magnet guns.

Harry dashed back to the other side of the wrecked artrak as the side he had used as cover got perforated. He took aim at the Cykots again, but this time, instead of hitting their eyes, he shot at their throats. This wouldn't kill them, but that's not what he wanted. The force from the impact jolted their heads upward, causing their green beams to hit the back of the Titanborg, damaging far more than his needle gun could hope to do.

More controlled shots took down all but a few of the Cykots. A slot opened on the side of the Titanborg's leg. This is what Harry waited for. He only had a fraction of a second to take the shot. And the moment quickly came.

The missile fired, but a needle bullet hit its tip before it left the launcher. It exploded, consuming the Titanborg and the infantry behind it. Harry kept his aim fixed on the cloud of fire and black smoke.

It cleared a few moments later. The Cykots were all down, but the Titanborg was slumped on one knee with its magnet gun trained on Harry. Harry swallowed hard. He was out of ideas.

A strafing hail of bullets hit the Dread Corpsman from above, jerking it to the side, and causing the burst from the adversary's guns to hit the ground to the side of Harry with rumbling thumps.

Harry glanced up as the Titanborg took aim at the long, narrow profile of a lone Javelin fighter jet. The Allied vehicle was indeed reminiscent of a spear. The Allied aircraft evaded the first few blasts from the Titanborg, but took a glancing hit as it blasted a concentrated burst into the armored enemy, blowing through its center of mass. It slumped to the ground and fell over with a boom.

The Javelin fighter hurtled off to the northern horizon, leaving a trail of inky smoke behind it. Harry kept his rifle leveled at the Titanborg until it flared into nothingness along with the Cykots. Disintegrated. Dread Corps never left tech or dead bodies behind. Even the victorious battles of the War of No Hope looked like defeats.

Harry looked to the sky and saw no glowing red Dread Doors. Maybe they'd caught a break. He risked turning on his radio again within his helmet. "This is Mang. Off radio silence. The Cykots and the Titanborg are gone. I have no visuals on other hostiles."

"Mang!" Braller's voice yelled in his ear. "Holy fuck! You killed every gods-damned one of them."

"Except the Titanborg. Is that Javelin fighter still with us? I owe that pilot a drink. He saved my life."

"He's checking on Petoltown, making sure no other Dread Doors pop up," Braller said. "There was a full squadron of ten Javelins. They ran into some Aesurs. He was the only survivor on either side."

Harry leaned against the charred artrak as the adrenaline left him. He wanted to vomit, but he fought back the sensation. He slouched down to his knees, his legs feeling like rubber. "Last man flying."

"You two saved all of us," Braller said. "I can't believe it. It was like you were... I don't even know. Like you were Starm him-fucking-self."

"Blasphemy," Harry said dryly, not really caring, but also not wanting some Propaganda Bureau jackass to jump down his throat about it later.

"Heh, yeah. Sorry. Look, Mang. If you ever–" Braller stopped talking for a few seconds. He returned with a more professional and discomforted tone. "Taskmaster Quentra needs to speak with you. In person. Get back here. Double time."

Harry groaned in weariness and rose to his feet on unsteady legs. "Roger. Heading in now."

Harry jogged over the grassland, blackened by the disintegrated Dread Corpsmen. The metallic wall and squat buildings of the bivouac base were all hastily erected. Sturdy, but not permanent. He reached the modular barricade door, which opened for him. No one cheered for him amidst the buildings. No one offered words of congratulations. Diana must have yelled at all of them to suck it up, not celebrate, because Dread Corps loved to return out of nowhere just when you let down your guard. He'd heard it enough over his year and a half of service.

Harry approached the open door of Taskmaster Quentra's command bunker. It was unremarkable by design in order to prevent it from becoming a target. He stopped at the doorjamb. "Knight Mang reporting, ma'am."

"Come in, Mang," her soft, prim voice ordered from the dim interior. "Close the door behind you."

Harry did as she asked. Diana Quentra sat behind a desk with a pistol laying atop it. "At ease. Have a seat."

He sat in front of her and pulled off his faceless helmet. The air cooled his perspiring face. He took in a deep breath of the air that reeked of smelted metal and industrial-strength glue. His eyes fixed on her pistol. "Diana, why is your side arm on your desk?"

"Oh, I was going to kill myself until about five minutes ago. Was working up the nerve."

Harry frowned at her in the dull, color-depleting light from the overhead lamps. "Because you expected me to die. And then everyone else to do the same."

"Yes." Her voice was distant. She placed her hand on the pistol's grip.

Harry lashed his hand atop hers, staring hard into her eyes. "Promise me. Promise me right now that you aren't using this on anyone but Dread Corps."

Diana's face hardened. "Remove your hand, Knight. That's an order."

"Promise me first, Taskmaster."

She slapped him across the face with a powerful smack. "I am your commanding officer. Release my weapon, or I will have you whipped."

Harry's ear rang and his face prickled, but he kept the flare of anger from showing on his face. He kept his hand clasped on hers. "Promise me."

She swatted at his face again, but he intercepted it with his free hand. "Diana. Please promise me."

Her arms trembled. She tried to lift the hand holding the gun and claw at his face with her other. She couldn't overcome his strength. Finally, she looked him in the eyes. Her expression was hard, but also earnest. "You have my word."

Harry slowly removed his grasp from her hand on the gun. He released her other hand that had struck him. She pulled it back and placed the gun in the top drawer of her desk.

They stared at each other for a long moment. Finally, she said, "How did you pull that off?" She gestured to her handset screen, lying on the other side of the desk. "I watched you through that while I gave orders to the base to reinforce our barricades, and figure out if retreat was possible, which it wasn't."

Her mouth pressed together in a thin line. "All while calculating the best time to kill myself."

She rose from the desk, revealing her very pregnant belly contained within her grey fiber armor uniform. She placed her hand on it. "To kill us. I would not let them torture me, or do something worse to my child."

Harry remained seated as she made her way around the desk, still moving with grace despite her advanced condition. "I watched you," she said. "Sure you would die. Killing one Cykot after another. Killing a gods damned Titanborg that the Javelin fighter finished off."

Diana moved closer to him. "Every time I send you out to do something impossible. You do it." She grabbed his hand, far gentler this time. "I've seen you bleed. That's the only reason I still believe you're Human."

Harry kissed the back of her hand. "I'm plenty Human, ma'am."

"Don't call me that right now." She moved to his lap. She straddled him awkwardly, but still seductively. "I wish this child was yours."

"Her father–"

"Is a dead asshole."

Harry chuckled at that. "I won't argue that."

Diana leaned down and kissed him long and hard, caressing his tongue with hers, exploring his lips. She pulled away from him after a few more sublime heartbeats. "I ask again. How did you do it?"

"Instinct, I guess." Harry brushed a hand around the braided crown of her auburn hair. "It's a knack. I just feel my way through it, like it's a dance I've done thousands of times. I practice a lot. That's a lot of it too, I'm sure. And some luck."

Diana kissed him again. "You and I are going to fuck each other silly tonight."
She looked at him with some renewed hardness. "Then I'm putting you in for
a transfer to Stalse Springs before the rest of this company pulls back to Ilasav."

Harry swallowed. "Because of this." He squeezed her ass. "Because we can't
stop ourselves."

The taskmaster nodded. "And they need someone like you there. Dread
Corps has been hitting that city harder than anyplace else. They need someone
who can do the impossible."

"I'll miss you," he said.

"I'll miss you more," she said. "But it's for–"

A dull whirring sounded from outside. Harry helped Diana get to her feet
by lifting her under her arms. Her belly bumped him in the cheek as he also
rose. Harry then ran a hand down the side of his sweating head. She grabbed
her handset monitor. The tension in Diana's face regressed. "It's the Javelin. It
came back. Made an emergency landing outside the barricade."

Harry grabbed his helmet and placed it over his head again. "Want me to
leave?"

Diana nodded. "That would be best. I'll join you a minute later."

He saluted her.

She licked her chops at him.

The subordinate soldier turned and exited the modular office. He strode past
the rear guards and the buildings flanking him, his mind still on Diana and her
near suicide. Perhaps it was a good thing that she was transferring him. Their
relationship confused him. Neither of them were entirely emotionally stable
either. Of course, who was mentally well after decades of war against an enemy
with infinite ranks that took no territory? The bastards just attacked and left.
Either successfully killing people, or failing in today's case.

Harry made his way through the door and met up with Braller. His fellow
Alliance Knight wore identical armor to Harry, identifiable by two red stripes on
his shoulder. Harry's metallic garb instead had four green diamonds. "Taskmaster sent me to meet the pilot. Wanna join me?"

Not exactly the truth, but Diana wouldn't make it an issue. She didn't tell
him not to meet the pilot after all.

Braller gestured to the smoking hull of the fighter jet. "After you, Mang."

The sky dimmed with low-hanging clouds that pressed in from the north. Had they been overhead during the fight with Dread Corps, they might have prevented this pilot from finding him. Harry ran out to the Javelin as the pilot climbed down a ladder that had extended from the cracked cockpit. The damage to the side was extensive. The fuselage was shredded, the wing battered. Had the Titanborg's magnet gun aimed a bit more to the right, this aircraft would have been obliterated.

The pilot's feet thudded to the ground. Unlike the Alliance Knights, his helmet showed his face through a sheen of transparent hard carbon. His eyes were dark and his features hard. "My comms gave out on the way back from Petoltown. I need to contact strat command. Let them know I made it."

"Our taskmaster is on her way out," Braller said. "Her handset monitor should have the range for you." Braller looked at the side of the Javelin. "How the hell did you fly that thing back here?"

"With skill and determination, army boy." The pilot glanced around. "Where's that lone wolf who killed the whole battalion?"

Harry decided he wanted to look this guy in the eyes. He removed his helmet. "That'd be me. And it was a depleted battalion. Before our artraks all got slagged, they softened the bastards up. And you saved my life against that Titanborg."

The pilot extended his hand. "Meve Harlander."

"Harry Mang." He shook Meve's hand. "Is Petoltown ok?"

Meve nodded. "Yeah." He frowned with an uncertain expression. "Yeah, they are."

Harry shared a glance with Braller before focusing back on Meve. "Talk to us, Meve. If shit's sideways out there, we need that intel."

"There's a lot more of Dread Corps that tried to hit the city before you guys reacted, before my squadron scrambled." He looked to the northern horizon. "Lots of wrecked landscape outside the city. You can't ever tell how bad since Dread Corp's people and gear disintegrate, but you can get an idea by the land. They ran into something they couldn't handle."

Meve's face tightened with apprehension swimming in his eyes. "I think it was Xax."

Harry's stomach lurched. The ancient robot that went toe-to-toe with Starm. That thing had a mad on for the Holy Alliance and everyone in it. He moved closer to Meve. "How can you tell?"

Meve pulled out a smaller, card-sized screen interface. He made a few swiping motions with his finger, then handed it to Harry. The image displayed burnt and trampled grassland. Something had stamped two distinctive footprints into the soft earth, likely after having landed from a great height. They were angular, pointed at the toes, just like Xax's feet.

"Shit." Harry stared harder at the footprints. "Oh, shit."

"Yeah. Took that with the jet's camera."

Harry handed the smaller device back to Meve. "Is he still in Petoltown?"

The pilot shook his head. "There were people wandering the streets, waving up at me. They looked relieved. They wouldn't have been doing that if Xax were still around." He looked at the northern horizon. "You ground pounders will need to secure Petoltown anyway, but you're not going to find Xax there."

"No, we're not," Diana said from the side. "Because he was never there."

Meve looked at her eyes, her belly, then her eyes again. "Air Master Meve Harlander. You're the commanding officer?" He offered her no salute. Air Navy Air Masters and Allied Army Task Masters were of equal rank.

"That's correct." Diana also introduced herself. "Delete that photo."

Meve frowned at her, obviously confused.

"The Propaganda Bureau sent out an advisory. Didn't you read it?"

Meve shook his head. "The Proppers don't always get messages to us. Or the Fleet Masters don't filter it down our way."

Diana let out a hoarse sigh. "Gods damned politicking idiots. All of them." She pulled out her larger handset monitor. "Look, the Proppers are all in my business lately. And they gave explicit instructions to redact Xax from any reports we send to Reapings Command. Don't know why. Don't care."

She thrust her handset in Meve's direction. "So just swap with me for a second while I delete this off your jet's computer. Please?"

Meve glanced from her to Harry to Braller and back to Diana. "Sure."

The pilot called in his situation back to a Steelclad called the *Classica*. Harry's commanding officer and lover tapped a few commands on the smaller handset, causing the image of the footprints to blink away. The two officers exchanged their comm devices back to each other.

"My people are sending a tow rig for me and my bird," Meve said. "Should be here inside of an hour."

Diana nodded. "You're welcome to come inside while you wait. And Harlander."

Meve raised an eyebrow.

"Thanks for saving my man."

Harry's breath caught in his throat.

She then gestured to Braller, then to the base behind her. "All my men and women." Diana pointed to Harry. "You. Once the flyboy leaves, you're on point when we scout out Petoltown. Got it?"

"Got it, ma'am."

She grinned at him with a visible hunger that she quickly tamped down. "Yeah, you got it alright, Mang. You got it good."

She walked away from them without another word. Harry tried and failed to not look at the sway of her ass.

Braller stared at Harry from behind his faceless helmet.

"Don't give me that look," Harry said.

Braller held up his hands, then turned back to the base's front gate. "I'll get back to my post."

Harry gestured a thumb to one of the modular buildings. "I owe you a drink. We only have distilled piss, though."

Meve shrugged. "I'll take it."

After they covered a few dozen steps to get out of Braller's earshot, Meve asked, "So. Is that your bun in her oven?"

"No."

"But you two *are* fucking." He stated that as a plain fact, rather than a question.

Harry looked sideways at him. "I don't know. The Proppers redacted that intel."

Meve laughed hard at that.

CHAPTER 8

Two Bi-Months Later:
The Morning of Hexember 25th, 1569

"*Arch Cannons!*"

Harry opened his eyes. His head swam in dizziness. His body ached. Someone yelled about Arch Cannons. He lurched up. Tried to lurch up. Hard heaviness pressed down on him.

He sniffed back blood. "*Think. What happened?*" He was in the HQ outside of Lan Buthe. Chavet was giving a briefing. Something about a bunch of baby Dragons getting massacred in Inparadis. Then the Arch Cannons. Then this.

The soldier sniffed back blood and swallowed its awful tang down his throat. Rubble buried him alive with a building on top of him. He coughed. No. Not a building. Just part of a wall. He had run to a corner on instinct, just like he did everything else, like he practiced it thousands of times, knowing it was this safest place. The least unsafe place.

Harry's lungs heaved. He pushed up with everything he had. The flat object pressing on him budged, but came back to rest on him. He shoved against it again, giving it more than everything this time. He growled out a scream of anger and pushed the broken wall slab off of him. Light flooded into his face. Glorious light. He lay in the rubble for minutes, just huffing in the dusty air and occasionally coughing. He looked at the jagged metal edges rimming his vision. The wreckage had ripped open his helmet. It saved his life, but it was now useless.

Finally, he sat up with a haggard wheeze. Coughs shook through him now. He steadied himself over the next minute, staring at the ash mixed with dust. Harry grunted and rose on quaking legs. His equally trembling arms pulled off his helmet and dropped it next to him. He looked over his shoulder at what had once been a ten-storey building. Two-thirds of it was a blackened hole. The rest was a collapsed pile of masonry, metal, and dust.

He spat out filth that had caked his tongue and cleared his throat. "Sound off if you're alive. Chavet?"

Only the crackle of a few minute fires in the scorched earth answered him.

"Ernest? Ryans?"

Still nothing.

"Anyone?"

Silence.

Harry just nodded. Gods damned Dread Corps. They took everything. Diana, Braller, and the rest of his old company were in Ilasav when it got hit. None of them had made it. Guilt plagued him following that, keeping him from sleeping much. He survived because he had been having sex with his commanding officer, who then sent him away. Now he saw it for what it was. Stupid, stupid luck.

He stumbled through the ruins of the complex. Nothing stood. Just a grey haze blanketing everything, making the daystar look like a dingy flashlight bulb in an all-too-dark room.

He kept trudging on unsteady legs, not sure where he was going, only sure that it had to be better somewhere else. He tripped against something. Another Alliance Knight, crushed at the waist by a toppled steel girder. That could have been him. His dead comrade-in-arms did have a gift for him, though. He squatted and picked up a needle pistol. Not much. Barely anything. But it was better than what he had before.

Another few minutes brought him to the end of the base complex. The dander in the air cleared. He could see a few hundred feet in any direction. Had to keep moving. Had to get to some kind of defensive position. Before Dread Corps came again. And they would come.

That's when he heard footsteps crunching in the distance.

He looked around for cover, found a slanted slab of a wall, and jumped to it. He aimed the needle pistol at the source of the noise. Two sets of feet. He clenched his teeth. Beads of sweat dripped down his face. He just survived a building falling on him, but this felt more dangerous.

Two figures emerged from the haze. One wore aerodynamic black plate mail armor. One of his arms was slightly longer than the other. A black sash at his waist blew in the breeze with a simple design of a gateway connected with a pointed arch. Dread Corps's insignia. His sleek helmet completely concealed his face, coming to a vertical, sharp edge. He held a staff with a grey blade taking up half its length, a halbask.

The other man wore similar black armor in piecemeal segments, covering his left arm and his right leg. His muscular chest was bare save for a leather sheath strap of an oversized, jagged, rusted saber hanging from his back. A gateway arch tattoo covered the right side of his chest. No skin or muscle covered the bleached bones of his right arm. It moved with dexterous articulation, like the arm of a Mortisi. Dust flecked upon his mane of shaggy black hair and the stubble on his face. He wore thick, mirrored sunglasses. His head turned in Harry's direction.

Harry wasted no time firing his pistol before the Dread Corpsman saw him. The precise hit from the bullet knocked the armored man's halbask out of his hand.

The bare-chested man made a squeezing motion with his outreached, skeletal hand. Harry levitated into the air, unable to move his arms. His armor crinkled under the pressure. He coughed weakly. He was done. No chances left. His stomach clenched in both fear and anger. This was not how he wanted to die.

The bare-chested man jerked his arm back. Harry rocketed forward and saw his haggard reflection in the man's sunglasses.

The Dread Corpsman removed his sunglasses and stared at Harry. His eyes were also grey.

The armored man said something in a dark tongue. He moved closer to Harry and scrutinized him.

The bare-chested man responded in the same unknown language. His breath smelled like raw sewage.

The armored man nodded and walked to his halbask. He picked it up and returned to Harry and the bare-chested man.

Harry lowered to the ground. The immaterial grip on his body lessened. The armored man presented Harry with the halbask, holding it parallel to the ground.

Harry tensely frowned at the armored man.

"Take it, survivor," he rasped. "Fight us and die on your feet."

In one motion, Harry snatched the halbask, sliced off the armored man's head and impaled the bare-chested man through the center of his collarbone.

The decapitated armored man fell over on his side next to his head. His blood sprayed upon Harry's face and arms. The bare-chested man fell on his back with his hand clutching the jagged saber sheathed at his back. The halbask remained in the wound. Harry let go of it to wipe the blood from his face. The weapon stuck out of the Dread Corpsman like a flagpole.

The bare-chested man's eyes glazed over as death took him. His face grew pale as he coughed up blood. He spoke his last words in Rathune. "Corsis... *he* found *us*."

Harry frowned at him as the final trickles of life ebbed out of his enemy. "What?"

The newly deceased man had no further words to say.

"Corsis," he repeated. "No idea what that means."

The strangers' weapons disintegrated into dust. The weapons of Dread Corps always annihilated themselves upon their users' death. Both adversaries' bodies vanished where they lay.

Harry recalled hearing stories of these two unnamed Dread Corpsmen. They challenged others to single combat. None had lived through the experience. None but him. These two were also involved in the deaths of countless Dragons and Murdrakes.

Another few minutes passed as Harry trod out of the ruined base to the knee-high grassland outside. A rumbling engine now neared him. An artrak rolled over a pile of debris. Its guns were all melted, and the front half of its chassis was charred black, but it was still rolling and running. The vehicle stopped and its top hatch opened. A pilot rose from it, his helmet differentiated from that of an Alliance Knight by its diamond-shaped eye slots. "You okay, kid?"

Harry stared at the artrak and the Knight. "Yeah."

"Get on. There's nothing else here for us."

Harry approached the artrak on rubbery legs. Elation flowed through him, not for seeing another Human, but for being able to get off his feet.

"That was incredible. What you did to those two bastards."

Harry lurched up on the back of the rumbling vehicle. He splayed over on his back, letting the exhaustion take him. "You saw?"

"Yeah, on long range display." The artrak pilot gestured to his vehicle's melted guns. "All we could do was watch. Then they gave you that sword thing and you killed them. Fastest, wickedest moves I've ever seen, kid."

Harry managed a bitter smile as he stared at the now cleared sky.

"Why the hell did that guy hand you his weapon? They had you dead where you stood."

Harry looked back in the direction that the two Dread Corpsmen had lain in the broken street, now out of sight. "I don't know."

A few shouts of joy came from within the artrak. Harry regarded the diamond-shaped eye slots of the artrak pilot. "What's going on?"

"We have reports that Dread Corps just evacuated Lan Buthe."

Harry coughed. "Good."

The officer shook his head. "They'll be back. They're always back."

CHAPTER 9

Five Years Later:
The Evening of Hexember 25th, 1574

"Glad I came back?" Avril asked.

"Very." Harry stared at her nude ass swaying away from him and grinned anew. Nothing made sense right now. He didn't care at all. He just wanted this moment to last a little longer. Just a little.

The ass's owner looked over to him, a few locks of her red hair dropping over her shoulder. The makeshift torches flickered with warm light. This cave was small, only half as big as his quarters back at the forward base. That made things cozy with the torches, the double-sized sleeping bag, and the bottle of Rakers, which was just fine with him.

She blushed for a moment before a grin blossomed to replace it. Mischievous, not contented. "I never figured you for an ass guy, Harry. Not with all the staring at my chest that you do."

"I'm an admirer of all your curves."

"I know," she said with a bob of her eyebrows.

Harry took in a satisfied breath. "I'm so glad we didn't kill each other. Heavens know I tried plenty of times."

She grabbed the bottle of Raker's Rum from Harry's knapsack and took a long swig. "I did too. Until that night."

Harry sat up. "In this cave. In the sandstorm."

Avril sauntered back to him and handed him the bottle. "And we came to terms."

Harry grabbed the bottle and took an equally large swig of the spicy but smooth liquor. It traced a warm path down his throat and into his stomach. "That we did."

"Those terms." Avril knelt next to him on the sleeping bag and gazed down into his eyes. She clasped part of the sleeping bag in her fingers, squeezing it tightly. "They're coming to an end."

Harry nodded. Both of them faced death as traitors if their affair became known by either the Holy Alliance or the diminished ranks of the Krians. And the fact remained that she worked for a sect that followed a forgotten goddess, long imprisoned by the empire he served. Each one believed in similar but opposing world views. Uniting Jeea under Starm's banner versus bringing down the Holy Alliance to prop up a mad goddess in Starm's place. They would not work things out.

"So let's go out in style." She kissed him deeply. He returned it and held her delightfully warm body to his. That led to gentle caresses that became more frenzied as the moments passed. To moans. To gazing into each other's eyes. She then mounted him and squeezed, moving up and down. The utter pleasure melted away time.

She looked down at him with playful eyes and winked at him. He sprang up and kissed her anew. They got twisted around until he took her from behind, both moaning, bodies moving in synch. They tangled yet again, and they climaxed while on their side, thrusting into each other back and forth. Both held on to each other as Harry went soft inside of her.

"That was..." He brushed her hair away from his face and huffed in a deep breath. "Stylish."

Avril chortled. She then kissed his earlobe and whispered, "Something to remember in the days to come." She pulled away from him. "I wish things were different."

"So do I." He looked at the half full bottle of Raker's. "Lots of unfinished vices."

She laughed at that. He loved the sound of it with her husky, alto voice, like music. Sassy music.

Both of them picked up their scattered garments and dressed again. Harry in his grey Alliance Knight, streamlined plate armor. Avril in her red and black leather gear. She lowered her head. "It's the fifth anniversary. I like what happened today better than what happened back then."

Harry picked up the bottle and examined it, methodically sloshing the brown liquid within it. He didn't need to ask what she talked about. It was the War of No Hope's last day. He knew scant details of what she did that day. The Krians and Grells formed an uneasy partnership, defending the Krians' lair. They prevailed, but the Krians were nearly wiped out.

He could have asked her to tell him more, but then she might ask him to do the same. The war's last day haunted him. Climbing out of the collapsed building, killing the two Dread Corpsmen, the name one of them said. Hell, he couldn't even remember it now. Collus? Carnum? It didn't matter. It was lost in the past with a lot of things, a lot of names he did remember. Chavet. Braller. Diana.

Avril looked deep into his eyes. "You've seen some shit, haven't you?"

Harry shrugged. "Who hasn't? That war lasted most of the century. It ended. But it will never be over. Not for us."

Avril kept looking at him for another intense moment, nostrils flaring. Her next words came with no connection to their discussion. "My father is in a coma. Dread Corps did it to him. I'm—"

Harry placed a gentle hand on her shoulder. "You don't have to tell me this. I'm your enemy."

She clasped her hand atop his. "No, Harry. You work for my enemies. You and I. We're... we're good. And I need to tell you. Because someone needs to know. You'll keep this secret. I know you will."

Harry looked at her with his mouth slightly agape, completely off his guard, but still choosing to let her talk.

"I'm freeing my goddess. I'm doing it either by myself or with help. I have some leads. And I can't let you, your tasty lips, and your tastier cock distract me anymore. That's why this has to end."

He tilted his head. He was supposed to get in her face, tell her she couldn't hope to succeed against the Holy Alliance. Celsis Kri would never escape her prison into which Starm cast her. He didn't. The War of No Hope had long ago knocked all patriotic fervor out of him. And he had a real problem reconciling the suffering his empire caused here in the so-called Unholy Frontier.

Avril picked up her horned helmet with its fanned rear, holding it in one hand. "Say something."

He tried speaking, but the words caught in his throat. He grunted to clear it. "Why are you talking like you're trying to convince me? We both agreed it has to end."

She looked away from his eyes. "But neither of us wants it to end."

"We don't." Harry let out a long breath. "Avril. Whatever you're doing. Please make sure I'm not anywhere near it. They'll order me after you if I'm within two hundred trecs."

"You and the flyboy."

Harry grinned at that. Meve knew about their affair. The pilot always asked for the sordid details whenever they linked up on leave. Meve had encountered Avril a few times in combat, and once walking in on the two of them in a cheap motel in Findenton. He just laughed and closed the door, letting them finish.

She patted his cheek. "Don't worry, Harry. It's nowhere near where they'd station you."

Harry swept his hands around the confines of the granite cave, nearly kicking over the rum bottle that sat next to the double sleeping bag. "They put me all over the place."

"They won't put you where I'm going. You save little people they expect to die. The Info Corps has a few stories about you. Little ones about an Alliance Knight who calms things down when he's on his own. Talks things out."

Harry gritted his teeth. "They don't tell the stories where I'm part of the army. I can't do anything then. People die. I've killed some of them."

She kissed his chin. "And it tears you up. You're a stand-up guy surrounded by low lives. Maybe one day, you'll quit. Find me again if you ever do."

"I could make things better from the inside. I'm already a Master Knight. I'll be giving the orders soon. Not taking them."

She gave him a wan smile. "And where do you think they'll put an ethical officer? The Bulwark? Making reforms to make right millennia of oppression? Do you think the Dragons, Titans, and Demons that run your empire would let that happen?" She shook her head. "They'll punt you to the fringe or have you killed in your sleep."

Harry gazed into her green eyes. "Maybe."

They kissed again, deeply. Holding each other. She dropped her helmet on the ground. They parted with a string of slobber lingering between them. Avril laughed and brushed it away. "Maybe."

Harry looked at the rum in the half-drained bottle and grabbed it by its neck. "To what could have been."

She picked up her helmet and nodded at the glass container. "To what could have been."

He dumped the contents on the sandy ground by the sleeping bag and dropped the bottle. It landed against a rock with a clunk. The glass chipped, but otherwise stayed intact.

"So long, Harry." She donned her helmet, then turned from him waving with twiddling fingers, departing through the cave's opening, illuminated by the light of dawn. She sashayed as she departed, accentuating her rear's seductive movements as she did it. "It's hard to part ways, but despite that, I know you love to watch me go."

Harry grinned and admired her ass one last time. "Find what you're looking for, Avril."

CHAPTER 10

Eight Years Later:
The Afternoon of Quintember 18th, 1582

"Taskmaster," the hollow, electronically distorted voice echoed from the smoldering street of dirt, flanked by modular buildings. "You can't hide."

Harry swallowed down his mounting anxiety. Had to stay cold. Grey Jack would kill him if he got hot. The plan half worked. He could work with half. Just had to make sure that Meve kept that fucking Rig jet from giving the bastard air support. Just forty-three seconds to go.

"You're being an idiot, Mang." The sounds of grit and pebbles beneath boots crunched from even closer. "I can see your beating heart. I hear your breath. Come out. I'll make it quick. Out of respect."

Like he had made it quick for that building of families in Findenton. For that fish market in Cape Camley. For that village of Engalians. Grey Jack knew Harry was in this empty complex of hollow buildings. He knew the life sign echoes they used to lure him here were fake. But he didn't know something about Harry's life signs. The very ones the maniac tracked.

The taskmaster licked his lips. "*Come on, you cocky fuck wad,*" he thought to himself. "*Come and get me.*" Twenty-nine seconds remained.

"Have it your way," Grey Jack said. "Die like all the other Allied rats."

Harry leapt out as the armored spree killer fired a red blast from the manifold gun mounted on his wrist. At the wrong modular building. In the opposite direction. Something continued to distract him. A cruel trick, but nice men died against Grey Jack.

Harry leveled a magnet sniper rifle, modified with two ultra-dense black diamond rounds at the prone enemy. He fired at Grey Jack's manifold gun first. The report echoed as the bullet hit the armored madman's wrist weapon, shredding it. Harry fired again as Grey Jack pivoted to face him. The second black diamond round ripped the manifold gun clean off Grey Jack's forearm, sending its sparking, burning pieces skittering across the white sand between the buildings.

Harry glimpsed the Keeper device that had broadcast his vital signs in the wrong direction and hid his actual location. It also projected a hologram of a Pale Chromatic woman with five girls in front of her ranging from three years old to seventeen. The woman, their mother, wore a warm smile with a short hairstyle of alabaster hair. The teenager looked disdainful and the other four girls wore forced but cute smiles.

A short sword of red-hot hard light flared into Grey Jack's hand. "You know."

"That's right." Harry loaded a third round into the sniper rifle. Fourteen seconds. "Crysto."

"There is only Grey Jack. Only death for Demons and their minions." He pointed at Harry. "Like you."

A hundred feet above Grey Jack, a boxy vehicle wavered into sight. The Rig had been invisible. Grey Jack controlled it remotely. Harry fired at it with the explosive round, which collided with the Rig's armor, doing no more harm than scorching its hull with a bright flare. Which is exactly what Harry wanted. Six seconds.

"I know where your mother lives, Mang. I'm going to kill her after you."

"No, you're not." Harry dove to the side as a buzz of high-caliber bullets cut into the Rig from above followed by a streamlined bomb. Meve's javelin fighter swooped just above it, with its engines now roaring to life.

Meve and Harry had planned all of this. The stuff that went wrong. Grey Jack was supposed to spend more time attacking the empty buildings while Harry sniped at him from afar.

And the stuff that went right. The deception and distraction. Harry taking out his manifold gun. Meve's silent dive bomb run from forty-thousand feet with engines cold to avoid detection.

Harry rose to his feet and loaded another two black diamond rounds into his sniper rifle.

Grey Jack sprinted out of the raining debris as his aircraft crashed behind him. He rushed at Harry, brandishing the glowing short sword.

"Shit." He recovered his composure before Harry did. Harry fired a round at his neck, but hit his shoulder plate, making a ping.

Grey Jack reached him and sliced the rifle's barrel in half. Harry swung the stock of the ruined weapon at his enemy's head, doing nothing to him.

Harry feinted back and side-stepped a searing hack that would have taken off his arm. He pulled out his sword sheathed at his side, edged with the same black diamond compound. It could last a few minutes against Grey Jack's energy sword.

"That echoer with my family's portrait." Grey Jack tried to press Harry back, get him to retreat, but Harry side-stepped and parried the attack with a sizzle of energy on his carbon and metal sword.

"Someone in Crystal Keep helped you," Grey Jack said while slashing at Harry. He ably deflected each hit, waiting for his moment. "I'll kill them after your mother. Her name is Lauthi. She has high blood pressure. Sings of Starm's glory when she talks to her friends about you. She enjoys playing castles with the fifteen-card variant. I know this and more, Mang."

Harry held his ground, still parrying each hit as Grey Jack's strikes grew more and more frenzied.

"You can't stop me. The Alliance will fall. Everything has to bleed." Grey Jack thrust his glowing sword at Harry's heart. "To death."

Harry leapt to the side with a diagonal upward thrust of his sword. The blade stabbed into the joint of Grey Jack's weakened shoulder plate, through the meat of his throat, and out the side of his neck. He widened his eyes at the sight of the maniac's ruin. "You first."

Blood spurted from the wound in a bright red geyser.

Harry jumped back as Grey Jack slashed his energy sword at his abdomen.

Grey Jack gurgled out something. A whirring sound rumbled from the side.

Harry couldn't understand the madman and he didn't want to. He backed farther away as Grey Jack faltered to one knee. He pointed at him and then gave Meve an upraised thumb.

The source of the whirring noise, the hovering Javelin fighter, leveled its forward-mounted cannons at Grey Jack. A barrage of metal ripped into his body for ten full seconds. When the fusillade ceased, Grey Jack's limbs were bent in unnatural directions and his helmet was caved in. The attack had not actually punctured the madman's armor, though blood and gore oozed from its joints.

A minute later, Meve stood next to Harry after he landed the Javelin fighter. "You were supposed to snipe his ass after I took down the Rig. Not get in a gods damned melee with him. I didn't have a clear shot and couldn't talk to you with the radio's silenced."

"He rushed me. Recovered faster. And you had a clear shot at the end."

Meve removed his helmet and ran his hand through his thinning blonde hair. "After you did one of your one-in-a-million hits through his throat. How the hell did you breach his armor?"

Harry shrugged. "Saw a weakness exposed by my sniper round and took advantage of it."

Meve shook his head, disbelief apparent on his face. "This guy had everyone on his ass. The Alliance, the Keepers, the Union Cities. He went toe-to-toe with a few Titans. Killed one of them. Survived a run in with Xax. But not against you."

"And you." Harry clasped Meve's shoulder and jostled it. "How was that dive run?"

"My nuts are still in my throat. It was well beyond terminal velocity. I'm just glad the engines came back on."

They looked at Grey Jack's ruined body for a few more seconds.

Harry frowned at it. "You know...."

"Yeah, I was thinking the same thing," Meve said. "I expected him to disintegrate. Like Dread Corps."

"Think his armor is booby trapped?" Harry asked.

"Has to be."

Harry squinted at something next to the ruined body. A compartment on his belt had fallen open, spilling its contents onto the sandy ground, a golden locket and two silver cubes the size of a thumb tip.

The taskmaster crouched and reached out with the flat of his sword and scraped the two cubes and the locket toward him. He picked them up and backed a few steps away, still unsure that Grey Jack didn't have a posthumous surprise waiting for them.

Meve looked at the objects in Harry's palm. "Open the locket."

Harry eyed the golden circular object for a long moment and determined that it looked safe. He opened it to reveal an identical holographic projection of the woman and the five girls. The dead wife and daughters of Crysto Hollak. "They're the reason he did this."

Meve nodded. "Fuckin' Horrinshal. We always have to clean up after them."

Harry dropped the locket into the sand at his feet. The image of the six Keeper females flickered away. "This wasn't clean up. This was throwing one mess on top of another." He narrowed his eyes at the metal cubes. "I think these are Keeper data cubes."

Meve jutted a thumb at the echoer down the street. "Think the colonel's gadget over there can read it?"

"Let's find out."

The soldier and the pilot strode past the vacant buildings over to the echoer given to them by Colonel Chella Crown, a Keeper officer who reached out to them through the Findenton black market. She wanted Grey Jack killed and gave them intelligence on Grey Jack's dead family and also donated this device that could fool his suit's scanning capabilities.

Harry looked over the echoer's smooth interface and found a cube-shaped slot on its side. He slid one of the cubes into it. A text page replaced the holographic image of the Hollak family with a title of "Manifesto". Harry read the first few lines aloud, "'I am ready to begin. My family will be the last to die at the hands of the Alliance. Dread Corps proved that an enduring campaign of terror can grind their war machine to a halt. I can be worse. I will be the nightmare. I will–'" Harry stopped reading it. "It's a war journal. Might have valuable intelligence, might be a lot of crazy. I don't want to read it to find out. You?"

Meve shook his head. "You trust anyone on our side to go through it?"

"No." Harry yanked out the data cube. He considered crunching it under his boot, but decided against it. Instead, he placed it into one of his belt pockets. "Let's see what the other one says."

Harry shoved in the other data cube, expecting more ravings. Instead, a map flared up in the hologram display. The heading at the top read, "Safehouse 5." Harry used the echoer's arrow buttons to scroll through it, very glad he was fluent in Jeean. It detailed Grey Jack's arsenal's capabilities, and existence of a backup suit of armor and a second Rig aircraft.

Meve stared at him. "We can't do anything with his gear. Our people would do something awful with it. Chella Crown would order a hit on us."

Harry rubbed his chin. He looked at the destruction wrought by Grey Jack on this place. He recalled all the other places he terrorized. All the people he killed. "What if you and I go to Hollak's safehouse, take everything out of it? Hide it someplace. Keep it for when we need it."

Meve frowned at him. "If either of us put on the Grey Jack armor or use his Rig, the world will fall on us."

"Then we don't use it unless we absolutely have to. You and I are the only two people who can know about this."

Meve clasped his hand against the back of his neck. "Gods damn it, Hare. I don't need this headache."

Harry looked his friend in the eyes with a hard stare. "It'll be more of a headache if we just walk away from this or let our side or the Keepers raid Hollak's safehouse. Or worse, if some scavenger finds it."

Meve lowered his hand. His jaw clenched for a few moments before it loosened. "Ok, you convinced me. Before we go there, we gotta line up some storage in Findenton. And no one can know about this but you and me."

"Absolutely." Harry slapped his friend on the shoulder. "We've got an ace up our sleeve, buddy. I hope we never need to use it, but it's nice to know we have it."

PART V: THE BURNHELTS

CHAPTER 11

Seven Years Later:
The Early Evening of Quintember 63rd, 1589

The light of day waned. Ed Burnhelt trudged after his mother through the sandy grass. The brownish red blades reached up to Ed's knees in places, nearly touching his shorts. Ed's mother, Kindra Shalai, kept a relentless pace through it. Grass waved above the leather links of her armor's skirt, and brushed the leather sandals laced to her knees. The daystar's light gleamed upon the intricately crafted, malleable bronze plates on her torso. The same lacing pattern also twined along her upper arms between her bracers to her chest plate.

Kindra led him toward a stretching white wall in the distance. The vast structure stretched from one end of the horizon to the other. An incandescent, azure haze hung above the looming wall. Both the haze and the wall encircled the entire island of New Grelland.

"Mom, what are we–" Ed's voice cracked. Dear gods, he hated puberty sometimes. He cleared his throat. "What are we doing?"

Kindra stopped her march through the wild field. She turned to him, her dark-brown eyes coring into him. At age thirteen, Ed already stood as tall as her. He would surpass her in height in a few bi-months. That didn't mean much. She still made him feel small sometimes. "We are doing something hard, son. Do you plan to keep whining about it?"

"Asking isn't whining."

She took in a breath, held it for a moment, then exhaled. "Your tone suggests otherwise."

Ed looked at her for a few more moments. "Never mind."

Her fist thrust at his face.

Ed deflected it with a precise swipe of his hand.

Now she smiled at him. "Good. You have been practicing."

"Fern and I go at it a bunch."

She kept staring at him. Her face was unreadable. "Fern."

Ed shrugged. "Een too. And you. But yeah. Fern and I get into it. You know, for fun."

She sent a kick at his groin, which he sidestepped. He then ducked an elbow at his throat as he jumped over her sweeping foot that attempted to trip him. He held up his hands before she could advance on him. "I give. I give."

Her face was alight with something dangerous. She looked pleased, but anger tinged it. "Your training isn't about fun."

"Yeah." He lowered his head, looking at the rust-colored sand upon his mother's leather sandals that laced up her legs. The many fine grains churned between her toes and mashed beneath his boots.

Kindra placed a gentle finger on his chin, pigmented a shade darker than his skin. She lifted his gaze to meet hers. Her olive-skinned face regarded him with the affection he remembered from the time that he was little enough to sit on her lap. "I'm sorry, son. It just surprised me. As long as you have structured training, I see no harm in you blowing off steam with Fern."

Ed nodded. Things had gotten so intense in the past few years. Both his parents had always told him they expected great things from him, both in his studies with a private tutor, and in his martial arts regimens with Kindra and Een. Ed's time with Fern was the only respite, even if it did amount to more practice, just less structured, and with far more jokes. Terrible jokes. A lopsided grin crept onto his face at the thought of Fern's latest wisecrack. Something about icicles up a pee hole. It was funnier when Fern said it.

Kindra just shook her head. "You have your Dad's smile."

Ed forced it away. He hated it when people said he looked like Vick Burnhelt. He wanted to look like himself, no one else.

Her expression grew serious again. "Come." She turned back toward the distant wall. Her long, curly, black hair trailed behind her.

They stayed silent for a time. Their feet crunched through the red grass and the rusty sand beneath it. The sweet smell of the Red Plains ebbed as they moved in closer to the wall. A spicier scent of something burning replaced it. The blue haze above the wall brightened into a glow. The sound of distant thunder rumbled from beyond the wall's border.

"You're going to see some ugliness soon, Ed. Something beyond punching and kicking. You need to see it. Do not look away."

Ed's brow furrowed. The Fire Well was on the other side of the Krullin Wall. A place of danger that threatened their homeland at every second. "What? Are you going to fight a Demon?"

She looked at him with the same perplexing and intense look of pleased fury. "You're a smart lad."

Ed's jaw sagged a bit.

She placed her hands on the bronze bracers at her wrists. She pulled two swords from nowhere. Her spatial sheaths hid the blades in a pico realm that orbited her armor. One silver sword was shorter and meant for parrying, a filv. The other was blue with a long straight blade, a vamberg. A blurring ribbon of light followed it. She called it Bluestreak.

Kindra gazed up at the top. Cracks of thunder sounded from the Fire Well outside the wall. She nodded. Someone at the top, one of the wall's sentries, heaved something over the side. The object plummeted into the grass-covered sand with a thud. The fall from greater than a thousand feet would have killed a Human. This thing was still alive.

It was a green-scaled body wrapped in chains with a writhing snake tail in place of legs. The brute's top half looked Humanoid with muscle-bound arms and clawed hands. He had a snake-like head with long fangs and slitted pupils within yellow eyes. The tip of the tail had a bony tip that looked akin to a mace with jagged spikes. It then made an unnerving rattle noise as the tail vibrated.

Kindra took a step toward the Demon. She spoke in a muted voice. One tinged with rage about to uncoil. "This, my son, is a Nagus Rattler from Forboda. He tried to breach the Krullin Wall as part of an army of one-hundred thousand. They failed. And now this survivor is here. As a lesson."

Ed looked at the Nagus Rattler's unblinking, hateful eyes. The Demon ignored him, instead gazing at his mother with dark malice. She raised her short sword, signaling the sentry atop the wall thousands of feet above them. The magnetic lock on the chains on his chest clicked open.

"Oh, fuck," Ed said, not caring about cussing in front of his mother. His mouth ran dry. His legs went rigid.

The Demon surged at them with its mouth open in a hiss, fangs dripping clear venom that sizzled on the grass below it. Kindra charged at the snake man with lithe grace. She caught its mouth with a horizontal slash of her filv sword. The adversary's tail lashed around to club her head. She pointed Bluestreak at it. A ray of hard light sliced off the rattling mace with a sickening slurping noise. The bony protrusion landed on the grass, gushing blood.

Kindra then thrust her azure blade through the bottom of the Nagus Rattler's chin and out the top of his head. The snake man collapsed at Kindra's feet in a twitching mass. Dead.

"Fuck," Ed said in a far different tone this time, his voice muted with shock. His legs now went rubbery. He swallowed back the urge to retch.

Ed's mother turned to him with the same pleased fury painted across her face with a few black splotches of splattered Demon blood. "This is but one of the things that wants us annihilated or enslaved. It would have killed you, me, and anyone else it came across had I not killed it first. This is what you train to fight, Ed. This and much more."

Ed looked at the inky blood spurting from the severed tail, the wound on the Demon's chin, and the top of his head. The blood rolled off Bluestreak in beads like it was mercury. Some of it had splattered upon her armor. Ed didn't know what to say. She moved like a dancer with ease, like she knew every step. His mother killed that snake man in a fight that lasted mere seconds. She made it look simple. Preordained.

His voice came out quiet, nearly breathless. "How many Demons have you killed, Mom?"

Her face went rigid, cold. Cracks of thunder sounded from outside the walled border. She waited for them to abate before she spoke again. "Millions less than I should have. The horrors out there are limitless. They will never stop."

That was not the answer her son expected. She wanted megadeaths. Genocide.

"Don't look at me like that, Ed. They're the monsters. Not me."

Ed looked into her hard brown eyes. "How should I look at you?"

THE NEW PLAYERS: ORIGINS 81

Her nostrils flared. "With respect. You owe me a debt, my son. Me and your father." She looked skyward for a moment before regarding him again with a touch less intensity. Shade darkened half of her face. "And your grandfather."

Ed frowned at her. "What debt?"

She gestured to the Krullin Wall, immense and immovable. "I'm about to tell you something that's going to discomfort you. Upset you." She sheathed her swords at her bracers, and they vanished. "And you're going to say nothing until I tell you I'm finished."

Ed kept looking at her with confusion. His mother was about to drop something very large on him. He could tell.

She kicked the top of some red grass blades before speaking again. "You were conceived out there in the Fire Well. In the trail right on the other side of this spot."

Ed's face soured in revulsion. He did not want to hear about this.

Kindra pointed at him. "Not a gods damned word. Keep listening."

His shoulders sagged, and he kept quiet.

"It was a plex hex. We needed the power from the Fire Well for it to work. Your father and I made love. While your grandfather maintained the etherea of the plex hex. Channeled it into us."

Ed's stomach lurched. "Benefactor was watching?!"

"Quiet." She beheld him with renewed intensity. "I didn't say I was finished."

Ed just let out a disgusted scoff. Inside, his mind buzzed with revulsion, imagining his parents out there. Twined and naked. With an audience of his grandfather. He wanted to gag, but one look at Kindra's dire expression made him swallow down that reflex.

She continued with the same gravity, not appearing to care for his discomfort. "We did it to give you a gift. A vastly generous gift. One we could only trust to our family. In about two years, Flames of Tumult will burn within you. Like the fires out there. You will have hyper powers on the level of gods and Dragons. Strength. Flight. Speed. Durability. Enhanced vision. The capability to vent the fire from your eyes."

Ed's head swam with confusion. Powers of a god. Parents in an exhibitionist fuck fest to give them to him. He repressed a shudder.

Her expression remained gravely serious. "We did it because we needed to. Because there are much worse things in the world than Nagus Rattlers. Things that we need to best. And we need it to be a Burnhelt who does it. Because we don't trust anyone else to hold the kind of power you will hold. You and your brother."

Ed swallowed. That somehow chased away his discomfort. It wasn't just him. "Matt?"

She nodded. "Your father is telling him as we speak. He will have different powers. He can channel the Flames of Tumult, control them, bend them to his will, use them to power hexes, convert them to other forms of energy. The two of you will become members of the Forever Guard one day. Our new weapons to win."

Ed waited for her to say more. When she didn't, he asked, "Win what?"

She pursed her lips for a moment. "The future."

He had the distinct impression that his mother had another word in mind, but chose something vague. He looked up at the Krullin Wall's white, flawless surface. "This is a lot."

Kindra covered her hand over her face for a moment. She did that when she fought off tears. She lowered it with her composure maintained. "It is. And it is your debt to your family. To me. You will use this vast power to make things better, not worse. You, Ed, must always be better. In all ways. In combat. In the choices you make. In the bonds of family. Of friendship. Better. That is how you repay this debt."

Ed's head swam with everything his mom had just told him. "I didn't ask for this."

That made her laugh. No mirth filled her voice. Only bitterness. "None of us *asked* for this. Our family does what is hard. It's who we are." She narrowed her eyes at the wall. "Let's get a little closer."

They walked within the shadow of the Krullin Wall. Its smooth white surface appeared flawless. A few jagged flares of blue flames crackled near the ramparts at the top of the barrier. Kindra tensely looked up at the wall while the furious azure light shined upon her. Her eyes scanned the top of the wall, searching for something.

Despite all the mind-bending revelations swimming through his head, this structure still amazed Ed. "I can't believe Dad designed this thing."

"It astounds me every time I behold it." Her eyes kept roving along the wall's top.

"It's protected us all this time."

Kindra nodded, still enthralled.

Sounds of distant thunder clapped twice more beyond the wall. "I don't feel safe here."

Now she stared at Ed with widened eyes. "Ed, we're never safe anywhere. Do you understand me? We are never safe."

Ed wanted to nod or say something affirmative, but he couldn't. He didn't understand any facet of his mother's mood today.

She huffed out a sigh. "It's been a day, hasn't it?"

"Yeah," Ed rasped.

Ed and Kindra finally reached the wall's edge. She placed her hand on its smooth surface and closed her eyes. "This wasn't just the site of your conception. It has more meaning for me. I was right here sixteen centuries ago when I reached the shore. Right here when that damned fire burned away the Mirror Sea. I was the last one to make it out of the water." She opened her eyes with tears welling in them. "I should have died, but your father saw me. Even as he assisted Benefactor in erecting the Field of Quandric, he saw me. He levitated me from the water and brought me inside of the Field."

She lowered her hand from the wall to Ed's shoulder. "Ed, I've run in the Trails time and time again. I've waged war against Sufrinzon. Your father, Een, Bander, Flynn and I have killed so... so very many in defense of New Grelland. All to keep this wall standing." She removed her hand from his shoulder. "And so will you and your brother. Do you know why?"

The back of Ed's throat felt like sandpaper. He knew the answer all too well. "Because Burnhelts do what is hard."

She placed a gentle hand on his cheek. "That's my boy."

CHAPTER 12

One Day Later:
The Morning of Quintember 65th, 1589

Ed tapped his thumb on the circular breakfast table, shifting his gaze from his mother to the tall, beautiful woman next to her. "So you're still not telling us why. The *real* reason why."

Next to him, Matt bit into an orange slice. His bloodshot eyes blinked in slow succession. He rubbed his hand up his stubble-covered face and his furled brown hair. Matt's skin tone was several shades paler than that of Kindra and Ed. He took more after Vick with that trait.

The elder brother spoke with the chewed-up orange in his cheek. "Pretend you're us." He swallowed the fruit with an audible gulp, placing its rind on the plate with the rest of the fruit in front of him. "Your parents just told you and your brother are both getting 'gifts' involving Flames of Tumult. Me in less than a month. Ed in a few years. You told Ed about winning the future. Dad told me about breaking free of the past." He leaned his elbows on the table's polished wooden surface. "There's more. Both of us know it. And you know we know it. So tell us how you would take it?"

The blonde woman, Een of Muné, gave Matt a soft smile. Her straight, platinum-blonde hair extended to the base of her neck. Pointed ears poked through her sleek mane. She leaned in closer with her blue, almond-shaped eyes widened. "I said much the same to your parents, Matt."

Kindra set her tea upon a saucer with a scornful furl of her brow. "I should have asked Bander here instead."

Een patted Kindra's shoulder, resting her hand on the woolen sweater's fabric. "But they convinced me otherwise. You know the storm is coming. You don't need to know which insect beat its wings to cause it."

Ed and Matt shared an irritated glance. The elder brother slapped his hand against the table. The sleeve of his green flannel robe ruffled with the movement. "I sleep like hell. I never remember the nightmares. Is this 'gift' the reason?"

Kindra snapped her fingers. "Watch yourself, young man."

Ed stood up, knocking over his contoured wooden chair. "Answer his question."

Kindra stood up, staring at her younger son. "Your chronic bad dreams aren't related to this, Matthew. And Edward."

He crossed his arms in defiance, knowing that he had severely irked her if she was calling him Edward instead of Ed. "What?"

She gave him a grimace, her brown eyes fixed on him. "Een and I look forward to training you in true combat. Not these play martial arts. The high stakes kind of training." His mother took a step closer. "You'll bleed, my son. One of those cuts will be for this moment right now. I'll let you know when it happens."

Ed exhaled through pursed lips. Good gods, his Mom could still scare him. He lowered his arms and paced around in a meandering circle, looking through the dining room's rectangular picture window at the meadow of brown-red grass and the evergreen forest beyond it. Maybe he could pull out of this. With an intentionally insincere smile, Ed turned back to them. "You both look very pretty today. Have I mentioned that yet?"

Een failed to repress laughter. It started as snorts from her nose and worked its way to her mouth as boisterous chuckles.

Matt leaned back and cracked a smile.

Kindra just glared at Een with a lopsided grin.

"It was the delivery," Een said when she regained her composure. "The words were stupid."

"They were." Kindra's face stiffened. She rushed past Ed and looked outside. Her brown eyes shifting from the cloudless sky to the forest to the grass. "It can't be."

Een stepped closer to them. Her muscles tensed beneath her white, silken gown. "What is it?"

Kindra pressed her palm against the picture window. "I feel them right out there, Een. They're in Ruby, Bellsu and Beo too. They're everywhere. Dread Corps invades New Grelland."

Ed and Matt shared another glance, this time tinged with fear. The younger brother's stomach tightened. The War of No Hope had ended before either of them were born, but they still heard people talk about it. Dread Corps attacked every nation on the supercontinent of Jeea for greater than four decades during that war. They sought neither land nor other spoils. Their only apparent goal involved terrorizing the people of Jeea in incessant assaults. The war ended in 1569, also without reason. No treaties were signed. No armistices silenced the cries of battle. Dread Corps simply stopped attacking. They withdrew into their own realm.

And now, after over twenty years, Ed's mother said they returned. Kindra's Perceptia gave her the ability to perceive evil intentions. Her predictions were sometimes vague, sometimes specific, but never wrong.

Kindra rushed to a white light-switch on the wall and opened it on a hinge to reveal a ten-button control panel with a green, monochrome screen above it. She pressed a combination of six buttons and leaned in close to the diminutive panel. "Vick, talk to me!"

A far calmer male voice responded from a speaker on the panel. "Go ahead, Kindra."

"Dread Corps is in New Grelland. They're near our compound."

Vick didn't speak for several seconds. "You're the first to report it. I'll contact Dad. You turn on the house's Q-Engines. Is Een there yet?"

"She is."

"Good. Fern is here with me. I'll be there as soon as I can. Keep them away from the boys."

Kindra clawed her hand into a fist. "I swear I will."

Ed's mother pressed a new fifteen-digit combination of buttons on the panel. White light flashed outside the house for a moment. The air outside shimmered for a few more moments. A transparent Field of Quandric surrounded the house now.

Kindra stormed from the panel to Ed and Matt. She clasped both of them by the sides of their necks. She gravely stared into her sons' eyes. "No matter what happens, you two stay inside."

Both brothers nodded.

Kindra solemnly released her sons. She backed away a few steps and crossed her arms over her chest. White mist emanated from two bronze rings on both of her index fingers, enveloping her sweater and her slacks. It cleared in seconds. Her bronze and leather armor replaced her clothing.

Een also crossed her arms to summon the same mist. Her silken dress gave way to red, formfitting, carbon armor. Piece-meal silver plate armor components covered parts of it with a brazier, gauntlets that extended to her biceps, and boots that extended to her thighs. A sheathed sword now pressed against her back in its sheath.

"The shield will hold." Kindra pointed to the window, which raised with a mechanical whirring noise. "Watch and learn. Your training. Your true training begins now."

Kindra climbed out the open picture window with Een right behind her. The glass automatically lowered behind them. The two warriors lightly stepped into the meadow surrounding the house. When they passed the transparent threshold, the air shimmered. Nothing appeared amiss. The gentle breeze still wafted over the tall grass, rustling the leaves of Drake-wood Forest in the distance. Neither one of them relaxed their stance.

Kindra grabbed the hilts mounted on her gauntlets. She pulled forth blades as if from nowhere, just as Kindra had done when she fought the Nagus Rattler. Een pulled forth her own sword from her back-mounted sheath. The Chan'la baslak was a straight, serrated sword. She gripped the silver weapon in one hand, though she could also grip it with two. Kindra dual wielded her filv and Bluestreak.

Three glowing red doorways with pointed arches materialized in front of Kindra and Een. Ed's stomach tightened. Within the churning space of the man-sized portals, Dread Corps's hordes poured forth.

Blue-skinned swordsmen with six arms charged at Een. Her body blurred with movement, the air rippled around her. Een now stood in seven places at

once. Her many bodies flickered as though a strobe light shined upon her. She
used Al'laan, the mental manipulation of space, to Strobe-Shift.

She took one step in front of a six-armed man and her form stretched around
him like an image viewed through an unfocused lens. With her next step, her
body crept behind the six-armed man. She skewered her baslak sword through
his head and stomped her foot onto his back. At the same moment, she stood
next to Kindra, parrying the metal claw of a single-eyed cyborg sneering with
pointed-metal teeth. Een also fought a man in black armor with a rocket pack,
stabbing him through the neck. She faced another one-eyed cyborg and a pair
of six-armed men.

Kindra remained singular. Her body swayed in a loose, rhythmic dance. A
shimmering azure ray gleamed from Bluestreak and punched through the eye of
one of the cyborgs. The beam ended in a point as an extension of Bluestreak's
blade. Kindra slashed the ray through a trio of six-armed men, slicing them in
half. A glowing trail followed the blade's path.

A squadron of fifteen men in black armor and rocket packs flew from another glowing gateway in the sky. They aimed shoulder-mounted cannons. The
beam from Bluestreak disappeared. Kindra horizontally slashed her sword in
the flying men's direction. A glowing blue vortex enveloped them, spiraling
them around its interior. Kindra slashed Bluestreak again. The vortex vanished,
flinging the flying men away. Most of them plummeted into Drakewood. A few
crashed into the prairie, sending up plumes of grass and dirt.

The dining room shook, rattling the teacups and the plate with the rest of
Matt's orange upon it. The cause of the repeated tremors now came into view.
A black, angular robot, standing taller than the trees of the forest behind it,
aimed a snub-nosed cannon from its chest at the house. Air wavered around
the cannon's short barrel before a conical shockwave surged from it. The blast
struck the house's Field of Quandric, which held firm in its dome shape. The
interior of the house shook again. Kindra's teacup fell off the table, breaking to
pieces on the floor.

Ed looked at the hand-sized control panel on the wall of the dining room. He
moved to it and pressed the intercom button. "We need help, Dad."

Vick made no answer. The house trembled again with another shockwave
attack.

"Dad?" The intercom remained quiet.

Ed punched the wall next to the control panel. "Fuck! Why'd they build this house in the wilderness?"

"You heard Mom," Matt said. "They're attacking everywhere. It doesn't matter where we are."

Ed tightly closed his eyes and rasped out a response. "I know."

The house rumbled again. The sounds of more cups and the plate breaking on the floor made Ed flinch. He opened his eyes and blankly stared at the flashing lights of the minuscule control panel. He didn't have the strength to look out the window at his mother again.

The tremor abated. Matt spoke in a small voice. "Dad'll make it. He will."

Ed turned from the wall to face his brother. A purple-skinned woman skulked a few feet behind him to the right. A black, coarse helmet encircled much of her head. She reached for Matt's neck.

Ed lunged at a chair. He tossed it past Matt. The chair broke upon the strange bony designs covering her body. She made no attempt to dodge it.

Matt flinched when he saw the intruder. He ran next to Ed. Each brother picked up another chair, ready to strike her.

She spoke in a husky voice. "I've come for you, son of Vick Burnhelt."

Ed threw his chair at her. Again, she let it break upon the coarse patchwork upon her skin.

Matt set his chair back down. "You know us."

The woman nodded. "We're here because of a Burnhelt's cursed love. Because of a broken Rule."

Ed grabbed the chair Matt had held. He hurled it at her with a grunt. This time, she snatched it by the leg. She flung it back at him. Ed jumped to the side. The chair crashed through the picture window, shattering its glass to pieces, thumping on the grass outside. The sounds of metal upon metal now rang out all the louder.

"Out the window!" Ed leapt through the broken window and landed on his stomach near the chair just past the jagged glass pieces. Matt hit the grass next to him upon the shards. Ed stood up, grabbing this brother's arm as he rose. Warm blood gushed into his hands. Matt had cut his arms on the broken glass when he landed. Ed pulled Matt to his feet. He looked within the house. Their shadows stretched to the house's earth-toned wooden wall. The purple-skinned woman no longer stood in the dining room.

Matt groaned in pain, clutching his forearms with each opposing hand.

Ed spoke at the same time as another shockwave from the large robot hit the Field of Quandric. The brothers leaned on each other as the vibrations shook the ground.

Ed spoke again. "How bad is it?"

Matt squeezed his arms tightly. His face lost all of its already pale color. Blood dripped from between his fingers. "I think I cut an artery in one of my arms."

Ed pulled off his T-shirt with shaking hands. The adrenaline rush left him. A sensation of heaviness weighed down his legs. He ripped the shirt in half. "Let go of one of them."

Matt released his right arm. Four deep cuts crisscrossed it. Red spurted from his wrist. Matt pulled out a few larger shards from the cut, making it spurt out all the worse. Ed feverishly tied his shirt around that wound.

"No, up higher," Matt said. "I need a tourniquet, not a bandage."

Ed loosened the knot and slid it up to his elbow. "Here?"

"Yeah." Matt's blood from his arms had now stained the stomach section of his robe. He extended his other arm. Blood merely flowed from it. Ed wasted no time in tying another tourniquet around this arm.

"You need help. You're gonna bleed to death."

Ed's eyes widened in shock. The purple woman rose from their shadows on the ground. She stepped out of the darkness toward them. She approached with intensity burning in her magenta eyes. Her lithe hands reached for Matt, beckoning him to her embrace. "No, he isn't."

"Stay away from me!" Matt screamed. His eyes rolled backward, and he slumped against Ed. Passed out from blood loss and fright.

Ed tried to heft Matt's dead weight, but he didn't have the strength. They fell to the ground.

The macabre intruder stepped closer to the two brothers.

Ed scrambled to his feet in another surge of adrenaline. He cupped his hands beneath Matt's armpits and dragged him along the grass.

Her stiletto heels stabbed into the ground with every footfall. She still held out her arms. "Give him to me." Her voice sounded softer this time, more tentative.

"Help!" Ed cried over his shoulder. He saw neither his mother nor Een in the swarming insanity outside the Field of Quandric.

Ed turned his head back just in time to see her thrust her hand around his neck. Her grasp was firm, but she did not squeeze. The purple woman traced her index and middle fingers of her other hand along the deep cuts in Matt's forearms. The wounds closed without even scarring.

He locked eyes with her. She stood up, forcing Ed up with her. "I'm taking your brother, Edward. It's your father's fault I'm doing this. Everything about today is his fault. Make sure you tell him that."

Her lips briefly twitched, looking ready to say more, but she held her tongue. Her fingers trembled upon his skin. Though her chitinous helm obscured much of her face, Ed saw more than hatred. He saw despair. She was going to take his brother, and he had not the strength to stop her.

"No." He clutched her fingers, futilely trying to pry them away. "You are not taking my brother. I'm not telling my Dad a gods damned thing."

The woman's magenta eyes widened. "I desire your blood. To devour your beating heart before your mother." She squeezed his neck far harder, strangling him. Her quivering hand juddered him. Pointed fingernails dug into his skin. "But–"

A blue beam stabbed into her helmeted face. Her head jerked back, but the attack did not penetrate her bizarre armor. She released Ed and backflipped upon her hands, then sprang back further to her feet. Black, bony blades telescoped from under her wrists. She clutched them like swords, though they remained attached to her forearms.

Kindra stepped through a vertical, eye-shaped hole in the transparent Field of Quandric. The opening closed behind her. She made no threats, no demands, no accusations. She charged headlong at the woman who had throttled her child. Their blades clashed together. The two women moved in a furious ballet. Every stab, every feint, countered by the other.

Ed knelt next to Matt. He lay sprawled on the ground in his underwear with his robe open. Ed gingerly touched Matt's wrists. Still completely healed, with no sign of harm. "Come on, Matt. Wake up."

Something screeched behind him in the prairie. Ed glanced at the battle where Kindra had fought. A giant bird of prey covered in white and purple feathers flared from the ground next to Een, a benu. Blinding flames danced upon the benu's body. She leapt onto a saddle upon the creature's back, somehow remaining untouched by the fire. The raptor cried out and took to the sky. It circled around to the many cyborgs, six-armed men and scaly Demons. Fire spewed from its mouth. The benu reared back and flapped its wings. Feathers streaked into the throngs of Dread Corpsmen as flaming daggers.

Ed turned back to his mother. Bluestreak left a swirling trail of light with its every movement. Dark, runny liquid ebbed from the intruder's bony blades. The drops of the liquid that fell earthward instantly wilting any patch of grass it touched. Kindra pressed forward with slices and stabs. The purple woman took a few steps back while parrying every strike. Ed remained terrified, though awe now dulled it. His mother protected her children in an unrelenting frenzy.

The ground vibrated three times in a slow cadence. He looked back, expecting to see the black robot. Instead, three larger metal giants marched from a massive, crimson gateway. They did not appear to be mechanical, more akin to misshapen suits of half-rusted armor. Their broad legs crushed the earth beneath them. Each possessed one arm twice the size of the other. A pair of glowing orbs floated within the giants' empty, open-faced helms. They stood far taller than Drakewood's forest canopy. They had to stand one-hundred feet tall, perhaps more. Years earlier, Kindra had told Ed of the Colossuses. With crushing, ponderous steps, the hulking trio marched toward the house.

"Oh... shit," Ed said. His mouth ran dry again.

Another shockwave pounded into the Field of Quandric. The black robot did not relent. It led the Colossuses closer to the house. Kindra was still locked in combat with the purple woman. Een's Strobe-Shifting bodies flashed about the battle on the ground while she also directed her benu to attack ever increasing swarms of scaled Demons. However, even Een could not be everywhere at once. More one-eyed cyborgs and six-armed men slipped past her, pressing closer from all directions. Kindra still paid the encroaching hundreds of Dread Legionnaires no attention while she waged her dire duel.

Ed grasped Matt's hand with both of his. "Matt! We have to hide. Wake up! WAKE UP!!"

Matt twitched and cried out, but he didn't awaken. His brother thrashed on his back. Ed squeezed his hand tighter while the earth shook. Rough voices bellowed all around. He kept his focus on Matt. "It's another nightmare, Matt."

Ed looked around again. Chrome joints of the cyborgs gleamed in the daylight. Fiery thrust of the armored-men's rocket packs gave off a dull blue smoke. The six-armed men did not have blue skin. Blue chitin covered them like the bodies of insects. The acrid smoke of the burning grass made his eyes water. Their harsh foreign words made no sense to him, but he knew they taunted him. Ed loathed beholding them with such detail. It meant they were too close. "It's another nightmare."

The black robot blew apart in a thundering, spherical explosion that consumed scores of flying Demons and men in rocket packs. Shrapnel from its body struck down several more cyborgs and six-armed men. The surviving attackers looked upward, as did Ed. Even Kindra and the purple woman ceased their fight.

A man encased in sleek white armor hovered in the air. Electric lights blinked upon a half-circular device in the center of his torso. Tiny gears clicked within a glassy gadget above his heart. A keypad on his forearm gave off a cool indigo glow from its circular monitor. A monocle lens over his left eye gleamed in the daylight. The only sign of the man in the armor was his purple eyes. He aimed a smoking, double-barreled shotgun at the Dread Corps closest to the Field of Quandric.

Ed grimaced at the sight. His father, Vick Burnhelt, last of the mechmancers, had arrived.

Vick cocked the shotgun. "Heathren," His electronically amplified voice echoed everywhere. "Leave."

Kindra renewed her attack on the purple woman, Heathren, before she could retort. Vick fired the shotgun. A conical flare blasted from its vertically aligned barrels. The six-armed men disintegrated under the blast. The sheer force of the attack hurled the one-eyed cyborgs in melted heaps. Vick cocked his shotgun again as the weapon's report thundered all about the landscape. Ed's father used the armor, the shotgun and countless other devices in the same manner a mathematician used a calculator. The tools of Vick's trade enhanced his considerable ethereal abilities.

The armored men in rocket packs and the winged Demons fled from Ed's father in a confused swarm. Those flying to Ed's left ran headlong into Een upon her majestic avian steed. Those flying on the right ran into something else.

A red Dragon soared toward them. Its leathery wings flapped with dull whooshes of air. It had a long serpentine neck and yellow eyes. A reptilian tail wove behind the Dragon in its own elegance. The creature had to be at least thirty feet long from head to tail. Slender, but muscular limbs stayed close to its body. The Dragon blew a jet of superheated fire from its mouth.

Een's benu released another swath of burning dagger-like feathers. The airborne Dread Legionnaires plummeted to the ground in burning heaps. Their bodies collided upon the burnt grass with pounding thumps.

Vick, Een and the Dragon flew toward the sole remaining foes, the three Colossuses. However, a fevered grunt from Kindra drew Ed's attention to a nearer conflict. The ringing of metal upon hardened bone near Ed never ceased, though they were louder. Heathren and Kindra's struggle lost none of its visceral desperation. Heathren took the offensive now. Her body blurred in motion, moving faster and faster, impossibly so. Kindra kept up with the intruder, but she faltered back several steps toward Ed and Matt.

The elder brother feverishly shook his head, but he still didn't open his eyes. Ed realized Heathren did something to Matt to keep him unconscious when she healed his cuts. He doubled over Matt. He couldn't fight Heathren or the Colossuses, but he could help his brother.

"Matt," he whispered against the chaotic noise about him. Ed blinked back tears. "Listen to my voice. It's Ed. Open your eyes, Matt."

Kindra stumbled when Heathren's bony blades scraped across her bronze armor. Sparks flew upon their contact.

Ed sniffed back runny snot. "Open your eyes."

Een's benu and the Dragon and unleashed another fiery barrage. The Colossuses plodded forward through it, taking nothing but superficial harm. The ground shook more and more with every crushing footfall. One Colossus attempted to bash the Dragon, but the agile creature flashed higher in a burst of speed.

Vick hovered back from them with his shotgun now strapped at his shoulder. He tapped an intricate combination of buttons on his wrist-mounted keypad. And the giants drew in closer.

"Open your eyes." Ed's voice trailed off. He gave in to sobbing against his brother's head, yet he still caught glimpses of fighting around him.

Another swipe of Heathren's blades cut through Kindra's armor, but she remained unharmed. Kindra wove her filv in a parrying feint. Heathren vertically sliced her blades like those of a pair of scissors upon the small sword. The bony blades sliced the filv in half with one jerking motion. Kindra dropped the ruined sword and pointed Bluestreak in a fencing stance.

Ed tried to speak to Matt again, but he couldn't form the words through his silent weeping.

The ground jolted again with the Colossuses' footfalls. The Dragon wove its hands and threw a glowing ball of electricity at one Colossus, charring it only slightly. Een Strobe-Shifted in a dozen different places upon their shoulders. Space bent and contorted around the Colossuses, yet they were not misshapen or disoriented in her Al'laan. They would not stop. Vick had long ago finished typing on his keypad. He didn't hold his shotgun again. He simply hovered before the three giants with a countdown displayed on his wrist.

Ed clutched Matt's ear and squeezed it. He coughed away his sobs. "Damn it, Matt. Get up! Get up! GET UP!!"

Kindra and Heathren crossed swords once again. Kindra matched the purple woman's newfound speed. She anticipated her every move. Bluestreak's glowing trail followed the blade in an intricate pattern. Kindra built momentum with the vamberg's every clash with Heathren's blades.

Vick pointed at the Colossuses and said, "*Magnetize.*"

The Colossuses lifted into the air and the unseen force pulled their limbs apart from the bodies in groaning, metallic jerks, getting drawn and quartered by unseen magnetism. Their empty helms popped off of their bodies. The hovering orbs serving as their eyes fell to the earth and shattered. Vick stopped pointing at their dismembered body parts and audibly grunted in fatigue. They hit the ground and shook everything again. The vast heaps of metal cast shadows upon the house and those within the Field of Quandric.

Kindra's momentum resulted in another feint that Heathren tried to parry, but Kindra altered Bluestreak's course. She sliced through Heathren's right elbow, severing the intruder's forearm. Black blood sprayed from the wound as Heathren screamed in pain. The severed arm sunk into the shadowed ground and disappeared.

The air shimmered again around the Field of Quandric. Vick fired his shotgun at Heathren. This time, a far thinner and precise blast flared from the weapon. Heathren sidestepped it in a blurring motion while clutching her stump. The Dragon let out another jet of fire, which Heathren leapt over to avoid. Een flickered next to the purple woman and hacked her baslak at Heathren's neck. The intruder sunk into the shadowy ground as though it were standing water.

Vick flew towards them with the Dragon and benu behind him. "Another Dread Door!"

A Human-sized, crimson gateway flared in front of the picture window. Vick blasted his shotgun at the doorway. Fiery breath from the Dragon's throat and dagger-like feathers from the riderless benu joined in Vick's barrage. On the darkened ground, Een haggardly rushed toward the Dread Door.

Kindra did not join her. She instead sprinted toward Ed and Matt.

"You are cursed like your father." Heathren rose from the darkened ground with the blade of her remaining forearm bared. She loomed over the two brothers with madness in her eyes. Their mother pumped her legs in giant strides, only two steps away.

Kindra reached Heathren as she pivoted. Bluestreak stabbed clean through Heathren's chest as the dark, poisoned blade impaled Kindra beneath her heart.

"MOM!" Ed screamed. Blood from both warriors gushed forth, red from one, black from the other. Some of both splattered upon the two brothers. A sickening scent of copper mingled with that of singed leaves filled Ed's nostrils.

The two women looked at each other. Heathren's purple-on-black eyes hazy. Kindra's brown eyes intense. Enraged. Heathren pulled her blade from Kindra's chest. Kindra tried slicing Bluestreak out of Heathren's flesh with a quivering arm, but it fell from her grip. The vamberg somehow slid from Heathren's dark gore and hit the ground. The black blood rolled off Bluestreak like quicksilver. Heathren fell on her back as Kindra shrank to her knees, teeth gritted, blood seeping between them.

Vick turned from the Dread Door. Nothing had exited its murky, churning interior. "Kindra!!"

"Goodbye, Vick," Heathren whispered. She sank into the shadow-covered ground. It swallowed her like quicksand.

Kindra shivered while clutching her wound. Her face twisted with rage. "That bitch just killed me."

Vick ran to her side. He knelt beside her and grasped both of her hands. "Stay still. You aren't dying."

He tapped one combination of buttons on his wrist computer. Blinding light glowed from Kindra's chest wound. She shook her head and shivered more. Vick entered another combination. She coughed up blood in response and put her hands on the shadowy ground.

The Dread Door vanished. Nothing ever emerged from it. The benu remained near the sight of the door while Een and the Dragon approached Kindra.

The Dragon walked on two legs and shrank in size as it walked until it was as tall as Een. "It was a distraction," the shrunken Dragon said. Its voice resonated with a bestial echo. "A distraction."

Een slowly sheathed her baslak on her back. She stopped walking. "My sister...." She clasped her hand over her mouth.

"Can we contact Dr. Achillius?" the Dragon calmly asked when it reached Vick.

Een still stared at them from behind. Tears flowed from her eyes.

Vick pressed more buttons on his wrist-mounted computer. "The blade was poisoned. She doesn't have the time to wait for him or anyone else."

Kindra glanced at Een with an intense expression while the Dragon and Vick spoke.

Een shook her head.

Kindra nodded at Een, who looked away. Stupefied as Ed was, he knew that simple exchange meant something, though he knew not what.

"Then, let me help you," the Dragon said. Both he and Vick failed to notice Een and Kindra's silent exchange. "Concentrate on mending the wound. I'll concern myself with the poison."

"Do it," Vick said. The Dragon's fingers wove while Vick keyed in another combination.

"*Poison Purge,*" the Dragon said.

Vick said nothing this time. The word displayed on his wrist-mounted computer's screen simply read, "*Heal.*"

Kindra shifted to her side as steaming mist billowed from the wound. Her shivering lessened. The bloody hole in the center of her chest remained open. "She killed me, Vick," she rasped. "It's over. Fucking over."

Matt stirred in Ed's hands. His eyes opened halfway. He wasn't fully conscious.

"No." Vick looked at the Dragon. "Do it again with everything you have. I'll do the same. Een, can you heal with Al'laan?"

"I'm a novice at it," she said hollowly, still unable to look at Kindra. "I'll do what I can."

Een knelt next to Kindra and placed her hands over the wound, whispering something, a chant, a prayer. Ed couldn't understand the words.

The Dragon cast his hex in tangent with Vick's mechmancy while Een kept pressing her hands upon the wound in Kindra's chest. Raw energies coursed through Kindra's body. Ed looked away as the light brightened enough to rival the daystar. When the light dimmed, her back arched and her limbs flailed. Healing mancy incessantly cascaded around and within her. Finally, she turned on her back when Vick and the Dragon spent their vast reserves. Een sat on her rear next to her. Steam rose from her hands. All looked at Ed's mother in a muted silence, devoid of hope.

Kindra looked at Vick with fierce emotion, even as her breathing grew shallow. "Let me see your face."

Vick grabbed the sides of his helmet. A pair of loud, automated clicks sounded near his chin, and he removed it to reveal his pale skin and sweat-laden blonde hair. Tears rolled down his cheeks. "Kindra, I can't help you."

"I know," she whispered. "I know." She gasped before speaking again. Blood oozed from her mouth. "Heathren. She'll be back. Three hearts. I stabbed one of them. Her arm will regrow."

Vick let out a single, bitter sob. "I failed you and the boys."

Kindra grimaced at him. "Vengeance, my love. Kill her. Kill her whole fucking family. We're close. The boys. They'll have the power. To finally win."

"Win," Vick repeated. "We can do that."

"Yes, love." She gently stroked her thumb across his tearful cheek, leaving behind a streak of her blood. Her bloody hand slid down his chest plate, leaving a larger smear. "Win."

Vick kissed her just as gently.

When their bloody lips parted, Kindra called to Een. "Take care of them, my sister."

Een removed her hands from her face, still sitting. She stoically nodded as the tears flowed down her cheeks.

Kindra looked at Matt, who still just half-opened his eyes, then to the Dragon standing behind them, and then to Ed. "My boys." She glanced at Bluestreak lying next to her and then back to Ed. "My wedding gift from your father... Ed, use it as I have." Her smile diminished. "Do what is hard."

Ed said nothing. Helpless sorrow suffocated all words.

Vick stroked her hair, anguish painted upon his face. "I'll love you forever."

Kindra coughed again, and her breathing became shallow. Her eyes intensely locked with his. "Win, love. With vengeance. Always vengeance...."

Her eyes closed and her body went limp. Vick removed his hand from her hair. He buried his face in her shoulder. And Kindra Shalai died.

CHAPTER 13

One Bi-Month Later:
The Night of Hexember 64th, 1589

Vick leaned his hand against the sticky bark of a forty-foot tall evergreen tree, one of the many majestic denizens of Drakewood. The sap stuck to his palm and his fingers. He closed his eyes and smelled the mix of pine needles and the sweet sap. When his eyes opened again, he yearned for any kind of change, but nothing did. Pale bluish light from the moon of Pathine painted the sky and the prairie in front of his abandoned, two-storey house. The white, angular paneling showed no sign of damage.

His sons and his ward no longer lived within it. Ed, Matt and Fern now lived in the Pyramid at Ruby under constant protection after Dread Corps's thwarted attack. He had built this house on the edge of Drakewood because he worried living in the cities made his family too easy of a target for their foes. He had another reason related to his guardianship of Fern. One he didn't want to dwell upon now. It was supposed to be a place of safety. Vick could not bear to set foot within it now. He could still smell traces of Kindra's shampoo, and the many lotions she lathered upon herself.

Pink light from Drathine, the smaller red moon bathed the landscape as well. The added illumination made the miniature craters from fallen Dread Legionnaires even more visible. All the bodies and toppled trees had long since been removed. The lavender incandescence of both full moons' lunar cycles marked the end of Trojis' calendar. A new year would begin in two days. It was supposed to be a time of celebration.

That was impossible, for other things also remained unchanged. Kindra was still dead, her ashes scattered into the wind from a particular spot on the Krullin

Wall. It was the spot where he had rescued her from the Flames of Tumult more than one and a half millennia earlier. The place where they had conceived Ed. His wife would never laugh with him again, hold him again, love him again. Sixty-four days had passed. Long days. The longest of his millennia of life.

Vick clenched his fingers against the sticky bark when he looked down at himself. He stood naked just inside of the tree line. Further within the forest stood another naked person. The mechmancer felt her gaze upon his back. He had to speak to her at some point. He betrayed his wife with her in this forest, and she betrayed her best friend with him.

Vick released the tree trunk and turned around. Een silently approached him through the moss and sticks of the forest. The eerie, violet moonlight fell on her through an opening in the forest canopy. Vick beheld her nude form, the most beautiful thing he had ever seen, even more so than Kindra. At that thought, he worked hard to swallow back the bile in his throat. "I made a mistake, Een."

Een moved past the lighted area, closer to him. Blue eyes regarded him tenderly.

"I took advantage of you," he said. "I had to feel something else. Anything else."

She reached for him and rested her warm hand on his chest. "So did I."

Vick placed his hand on her wrist, smearing sap upon it. Neither of them noticed.

"I can't do this again," Vick said. "I can't use you like this."

"You're not using me." Een placed her other arm around his neck and kissed his cheek. "That was how it started. Right there on your face. I was the one who did it. Not you."

"And I didn't stop you."

They tightly hugged each other. "I can't do this again," Vick repeated.

The two mourners held each other for several silent minutes. Neither shed tears through the embrace. Vick didn't know about Een, but he had long since run out of them.

"You have to let her go," Een whispered at last.

Vick released her and stepped back after she lowered her arms. "What does that mean?"

"You can't let Kindra's loss rule your life."

Vick frowned at her. The shadows from the trees darkened her face.

She rubbed some of the sweet-smelling sap from her wrist. "New Grelland needs you as it always needs you. If you focus on your dead wife, you lose focus on your great nation. It's cruel of me to speak of this, but it's also true. You are the only mechmancer left after the Eruption. Mechmancy is the key to New Grelland's defense. You don't have the luxury to mourn her anymore."

The blood rushed to Vick's head in a fit of fury. "I was married to her for almost seven centuries, Een!"

"And you abstained from wedding her for another nine centuries before that," Een said calmly. She rubbed the remaining sap from her wrist. "Tell me why."

Vick turned his back to her and regarded his empty house. The lights would have been on before Dread Corps ruined his life. Somehow, it made him glad that they did not illuminate the darkness now. He spoke again when he regained his temper. "Because of everything. Because of *him*."

Een stepped next to him, looking at the house she had once defended. "Neither of you had time for matters of the heart. Not with the armies from Decadia, Sufrinzon, Forboda, and the rest pouring at us from all directions. And him."

Vick didn't want to say Corsis's name, not because of his surveillance, but because the fiend had Kindra killed. Saying it hurt too much right now.

Een glided her hand into his and squeezed it. The remaining sap on his hand now glazed her palm. "Do you think Dread Corps will let us be while you recover?"

"They haven't attacked us since the day Heathren took her from me. From us."

"That could change. And even if they don't attack again, what about our enemy within our own realm? You've read the intelligence reports on the Holy Alliance. They have plans to upgrade their machines of war. Who do you think they will focus on?"

"Crystal Keep and the Union Cities," Vick said.

"And then New Grelland and Mun'la. We cannot let the city-states in Old Zivone fall to the Holy Alliance. We need you inventing and maintaining New Grelland's weapons."

Vick tried to release her hand, but she wouldn't let go. He squeezed it instead. "She and I were already planning our seven-hundredth anniversary in 1601. We wanted to go sailing in the Nor'Ocean."

"I need to tell you something." Een paced around to face Vick. She still held his hand. "Maybe you noticed, maybe you didn't, but I have always been infatuated with you."

Vick ran his finger up one of her pointed ears. "I noticed before I married Kindra, not after."

"I hid it better after. Kindra still noticed, of course. If it were anyone other than me, I'm sure she would have acted differently. But it *was* me." She paused, obviously discomforted with what she intended to say. "She told me about the vendetta on the Burnhelt family."

"Heathren called it a curse." Vick bit his lip. "Her family makes it a point to make it seem destined."

Een shook her head. "It's not. It's him. And his family." The Chan'la paused with her lips tight. She spoke again a few moments later. "Kindra made me swear something to her in our blood."

Een stepped closer to Vick. He felt her unsteady breath on his chin. "She made me promise to make you happy if something ever happened to her."

"That's a lie!" Vick pushed her away. "Kindra would not say that."

Een didn't approach him this time. She crossed her arms and looked away. "You're right. She didn't say that." The Chan'la then locked eyes with him. "She made me promise to make you *forget* her."

"No," Vick whispered.

"It's true. You know it's true."

Vick punched his fist against the tree, gashing his knuckles. He rubbed the raw abrasions for several moments. "It's just like her. Always thinking I was too fragile."

He looked upward at the moonlit sky. "We both have children, Een. You had Tamona the same year that Kindra had Matt. Our children played together when Tamona visited you. I know mine won't like the idea of us together."

"My child sees me more as a fellow Chan'la, rather than a mother. She would have no problems."

"I've never understood why you let the Guardian Mothers raise her. She was your child, not theirs."

"It is our custom. As you'll recall, I hated being 'banished' from my daughter for lack of a better term."

"I remember. I saw how you looked at Kindra when she held Matt as a baby. It tore you apart."

"It did," she said in a muted whisper. She then spoke far more loudly. "But I was needed more here in New Grelland as well. You, Kindra, and Bander helped me through it."

"As well as we could." Vick looked at her again. Her beauty was maddening. She had to know that. He growled out a sigh. "What do you see in me, Een? I don't get it. You Chan'la don't need men. You swim in the Divinity Pools to impregnate yourselves. You only give birth to daughters who are raised by the Guardian Mothers. I know for a fact that a fair number of Chan'la don't care for men on any level. What do you need me for?"

Een tilted her head with a bemused expression. "You are the smartest, most dedicated person I've ever met. Your lifespan is vast, like mine and the rest of my kind. Your passion has always inspired me. And far few Chan'la disdain the company of men than you would think. Especially those like myself who were *transformed* by Muné rather than being *born* of Chan'la mothers. I need you for all those reasons and more." Een approached him again. She laid her hand over his heart. "I need you because no one else will do. Not for me."

"Een... he won't let us be together. Loving a Burnhelt isn't safe."

"Kindra took her chances. I can too."

He gingerly lifted her hand from his heart. "But I can't. Every time we touch, it feels like betrayal."

She squeezed his hand with both of hers. "It will pass."

"Maybe it will, but I can't lose you like I lost her. I can't let it happen. I can't give you my heart. I need you too much as my friend." He lost himself in her eyes. He wanted to stare into them all night. Her presence was infectious. "I think it's best if we stay away from each other for a while."

She kissed him on the same spot on his cheek. "You need time. I should have waited. I've waited for centuries. I can wait a little longer."

Vick released her hands. "Don't wait for me. Don't let me wreck your happiness."

"You'll come around." She stroked her hand up the side of his cheek's stubble. "I have faith in you, Vick." She walked back into the forest to find her shed clothing.

Vick averted his eyes from her. He looked at his abandoned house again. He thought of the many good times he had within it. He thought of the wife whose memory he betrayed. "I can't let you go, Kindra. Not yet."

CHAPTER 14

Two Years Later:
The Afternoon of Blite 21st, 1591

A snapping, hissing torrent of unnatural flames erupted from Ed's eyes. He stared upward, venting the zigzagging energy at the interior of a mirror-like dome, a thousand feet above him. Blue tinged everything in his line of vision. Ed quaked. A frigid chill gripped his entire body, like someone injected ice water into his veins. The unrelenting blast flared without end. Ed ground his teeth. The pressure behind his eyes intensified.

"Take control of it, Ed," Matt said. From behind, the elder Burnhelt brother pressed his fingers against the temples of Ed's head.

"How?! I'm fucking shooting fire out of my eyes!" The azure blast roared out louder. The spicy scent Ed associated with the Krullin Wall and the Fire Well hung in the air. He tried to shut his eyelids, but they stayed open. "I can't stop it!"

"You can." Matt maintained his hold on Ed's skull. "Think of it like flexing a muscle. One that you've never used."

Ed shivered more violently. He bit his lip, grunting in exertion. He focused on the shiny dome's interior high above them. The Gift Sphere completely enveloped them. A flat, mirror-like floor bisected its horizontal hemispheres. The massive chamber compressed space within its confines. It took up far less space on the outside. Vick had built the contained environment as part of his massive underground lab, a few trecs from the Burnhelts' abandoned house.

It absorbed Ed's electric flames instead of reflecting them. The blast ended at the border. It didn't penetrate. It wasn't uncontrollable.

At that realization, the blazing torrent instantly ceased. Ed collapsed to his knees with his eyes shut tight. Matt released his head. Frigid tears ebbed down his cheeks. He crossed his trembling arms close to his chest. "Matt, please tell me that's the worst of it."

"I have no idea. It happened differently for me." Only the elder brother could risk occupying the Gift Sphere with Ed. He long since mastered his control of the eerie fire. Matt easily repelled the flames from touching him.

Ed risked opening his eyes. Azure still tinged his vision, but no fiery rays shot forth. He glanced over his shoulder at his brother. Glaring white light shined within his torso, too bright to bear. He looked away. "You're lit up like the daystar."

Matt paused for a moment, looking around the colossal, vacant interior. "You must be seeing something in the ethereal spectrum. Things look normal to me."

The air shimmered to Ed's left. Dark shades of indigo and aqua spiraled around Vick, obscuring most of his body. He had observed from the outside the Gift Sphere until now. "It's the Xeno wavelength."

Ed turned to his father, still shivering. "It's different now. Green."

Vick crouched in front of him, though Ed couldn't see him within the swirling aura. "The Haloi wavelength." He reached around Ed's head and placed circular goggles over his eyes. The chaotic, emerald churning gave way to Vick's concerned face. He wore a quilted white jacket over a T-shirt. A hole was worn in one knee of his black jeans. His jaw clenched while he regarded his youngest son. "Things look normal now?"

Ed turned to regard Matt. Something pushed against his motion, like he moved through hot tar. Matt also appeared as he had before, clad in a brown vest with a scruffy, unshaven face and bloodshot eyes. "I can see fine."

He looked at the grey bodysuit covering all but his head. The resistance impeded his movement again. White circuit lines crisscrossed the exterior, glowing slightly. The line designs didn't exude light earlier. "The suit is slowing me down."

Vick pointed a pen-sized device at each of Ed's eyes. "Good. It's the only thing keeping your body from hyper accelerating or accidentally knocking off someone's head. Your perception of time appears the same, so that means the gaseous ultra computer we're breathing is keeping up with your nervous system." His father's face remained tense. "Still cold though?"

"Yeah."

Vick pulled out a triangular gadget with a glassy surface from his jacket's pocket. He tapped his fingers on two of its edges. The inner coldness diminished, though no warmth filled its absence.

Ed rose to his feet. "Thanks."

Vick pocketed both devices in his side pockets. "Okay. Hans, I want a second opinion before I let the others in here."

Another person materialized a few feet beyond Vick and Matt with a shimmer of the air. A smooth visor of mirror-like reflective glass covered his face from his forehead to the bottom of his jaw. No hair covered the rest of his head. He wore a white lab coat with green, loose fitting scrubs. Ed still wasn't used to Dr. Achillius's upgraded, flesh-like body. He looked far more robotic before 1590. The only Human part of him was hidden behind his faceplate. The rest had burned away long ago in the Eruption. He spoke with a hollow voice, like it reverberated through a tin can. "Let's have a look."

Ed looked at his stretched, distorted reflection in the doctor's featureless faceplate. "Hey, Doc. I never knew your first name was Hans."

Dr. Achillius gently pressed his right hand's fingers over Ed's heart. "Doc has always been fine, Ed."

Vick tapped his foot against the reflective floor. "What do you think?"

"Ed flash fried all the nanomachines I injected into him." The cybernetic physician pressed the fingers of his left hand upon Ed's forehead. "We're lucky you didn't panic too terribly, young man."

His concealed face turned back to Vick. "No side effects."

Vick exhaled with relief on his face. "Thank the Protector."

Ed popped his lips. "Now what?"

Three more people appeared next to Matt upon the Gift Sphere's reflective floor. A tall, statuesque girl in white, silken clothes rushed to Ed. Her pointed ears looked just like those of Een, her mother. She also inherited Een's platinum-blonde hair, though it extended much farther down her back. Tamona's milky-white eyes saw nothing. Her acute Perceptia allowed her to perceive her surroundings better than sight. She hugged Ed in a tight embrace. "It was as though the Fire Well itself burst out of you. It was incredible." She squeezed his hand. "And horrible."

"I wasn't a fan of it." The suit resisted Ed's attempt to fully return her embrace.

She released him. Her sightless eyes vacantly fixed on his eyebrows as she smiled.

"Now, that's just sweet." Another newcomer leaned his elbow on Matt's shoulder. His bushy blonde hair furled around his head. He stood as tall as Ed, but he was more lithe. He wore jeans and a blue T-shirt with a circular target printed in its center. Vick took Fern in as a ward when he was orphaned as an infant. He was technically a foster brother, but Ed more often just called him his best friend. "Really, it is."

Matt pushed Fern's elbow away.

Unfazed, Fern stepped toward Ed and Tamona. His reflection on the floor touched Ed's feet. He shook his head with a confused expression, badly masked with a grin. "So?"

Ed looked at his friend with a raised eyebrow. "So what?"

Fern rubbed the back of his head, not speaking for a bit. Finally, he blew out a sigh through flapping lips. "Ok, I got nothing. Congratulations. You've struck me speechless."

"Yet you're still talking." Bennet Burnhelt approached his grandson from behind Fern. Ed and Matt, however, did not call him grandpa or grandfather. They called him by his title as leader of the Grells, as nearly everyone else did as well.

"Benefactor." Ed straightened up his stance.

While Vick and Matt both inherited his pale complexion, Ed got his icy-blue eyes. Unlike any of his descendants, scars marred his entire body. His dark blue uniform concealed all of them, but two on his face. One old gash extended from the left side of his forehead to the right side of his nose. The other ran vertically down the left side of his face. The scars intersected over his left eye. Miraculously, it remained intact. His bushy white hair extended to the middle of his neck. Despite his white hair and scars, he looked to be in his late thirties or early forties. He was actually just over forty-one *centuries* old.

"This will not be easy, Ed. Matt's hyper powers granted him external control of the Flames of Tumult. They now burn within you. You are transformed." He held his hands behind his back. "You must learn to control it without your father's suit and the Gift Sphere. We will train you in thinking, in fighting."

Benefactor paced in a meandering circle. "Your nation, your family, depends on you."

Ed murmured the words his mother once told him. "Do what is hard."

"That you will." The grandfather gestured around the bisected, reflective sphere. "But you must also be smart while you do the hard things." He brought his arm down, locking eyes with Ed. "You will learn that as part of the Forever Guard. Like your mother."

Ed swallowed hard. The stories of the Forever Guard's exploits numbered into the hundreds and spanned millennia. They toppled entire Nether Realms. They saved New Grelland from the fires of the Eruption. If the sky should fall, they would hold it upon their shoulders.

Long ago, Benefactor fought as one of them before he ascended to a position as Leader of the Grells following the Eruption. Kindra also proudly served with them before her death, as did others before Ed's time.

"You want me to take her place?"

"She gave you her sword to use as she did. That means standing with Flynn, with Een, with Bander, with your father, and with your brother."

Ed looked at Matt, who just shrugged. "It's the family business."

Benefactor gave his elder grandson a crooked grin before turning his attention back to his younger grandson. A faint azure glow emanated from his eyes. He levitated into the air, ascending thirty feet above the glossy floor. Benefactor possessed vast ethereal power as a mastermancer. "Ed, come up here. Step in the air."

The younger Burnhelt brother lifted his foot and stepped upon the thin air. His mother forewarned him he would gain the ability to fly, but she didn't say how. His insides lurched. He defied gravity, standing in the air. His foot tapped on what felt like an invisible, spongy platform, akin to tall grass on soft soil. He crouched down, waving his hands beneath his feet. He met no hindrance.

"You're creating your own relative gravity." Vick's stance relaxed. The worry in his face regressed. "You're doing fine."

Ed took ten more steps into the air. He looked down to Tamona, who still gazed forward, then to his father, his brother, his best friend, and his doctor. His reflection on the shiny floor appeared smaller. The white circuit line on his clothing glowed brighter.

"Keep moving." Benefactor ascended another five-hundred feet to the top of the curved ceiling.

Ed now broke into a run, bounding up what felt like stairs. His body suit pushed against him. He pushed back harder. The air rushed around him. A grin grew over his lips. He instantly stopped next to his grandfather, standing hundreds of feet above the floor. "I could get used to this."

"I hope you do." Benefactor bobbed slightly in his stationary position, contrasting Ed's complete stillness. "It will take much time."

The younger Burnhelt brother touched the top of the dome's reflective ceiling, gliding his fingers along its polished surface. "Yeah. Not looking forward to being stuck in here." He looked down at those still on the floor, tiny from this vantage point. "Heathren." Ed spoke the name of the woman who killed his mother with a muted rasp. "She knew about our hyper powers. That's why she came after us before they manifested. Tell me more about her."

The Leader of the Grells lowered his head. "We'll talk of her another day."

The grandson shook his head with a muted, bitter chuckle. "No actual answers. Nothing's changed."

Benefactor floated closer to him. "You'll get answers in time. I guarantee you will dislike them." A faint grin crossed his lips. "In the interim, your training begins. Steel yourself." The Leader of the Grells descended toward the floor far below their feet. "The future is dark. Pray for the courage to tread through it."

CHAPTER 15

One Year Later:
The Morning of Blite 55th 1592

"Today's the day," Ed whispered to himself. He sat on the edge of a cot with his elbows on his knees. The cushioning on his rear felt like it was a feathered bed. The hard-light hologram made soft things just easily as the obstacle courses he'd run over the past year and fifteen days.

He scoffed to himself at that time measurement. Yes, just over a year had passed. His body was sixteen. He still had a couple more inches to grow. His voice still cracked every now and again. But it hadn't been a year for his mind. He had thought so fast during the first few bi-months that he had lived thirteen relative years. He spent that time not only learning to decelerate his perceptions but also honing his skill as a swordsman, at using his hyper powers, at thinking on his feet, mastering tactics in multitudes of simulated environments. Still, not everything felt like vast tracts of time had passed. The death of his mother still felt like it had just happened days ago. It haunted him at the edges of his thoughts, of his nightmares.

Ed had learned to push it aside during the last three relative years. This stretch of time moved slower while he studied and trained through the Sphere's many lessons. He also taught himself logic exercises and meditations he could think through at hyper speeds, thinking through hundreds of ways to interpret situations and people's actions, and his own thoughts and emotions. It allowed him to work out his mental state, keep himself focused as he went through the drudgery of this exile from reality.

He took solace that he wasn't completely isolated. Fern and Matt paid him virtual visits from time to time as he got better at shifting his sense of time from hyper levels down to something closer to standard Human level. Tamona showed up infrequently as well. She, too, was mired in her own training with the Chan'la. The visits of one or more of the trio were every other day for them, and every few weeks for Ed. To him, he had spent half his life in this Sphere. This actual year and a couple of weeks. He had mastered shifting between sped up reality back to the slower "true" reality. He glared at the concave inner walls of the Sphere. It was time to leave.

A rectangular door opened along the curved interior of the Sphere. Benefactor entered. He had done that many times before as a sped up hologram. Not this time. This time, it was actually him. He strode over the empty few hundred yards and stood before Ed. "Light up your eyes, please."

Ed did as his grandfather asked. The world within the Sphere shifted to the soothing shade of blue. His eyes blazed with fire.

Benefactor squinted at his eyes, scrutinizing something. "Excellent. The energy signature is unique against your retinas. I can use this for verification."

Ed's eyes ceased glowing and his vision went back to the standard palate of color. "I take it you're worried about imposters, shape shifters, stuff like that."

Benefactor nodded. "Before you depart this gilded cage, I thought it best to talk. Just you and me."

Ed just crossed his arms, waiting for Benefactor to say more.

"I'm giving you some answers. About Heathren. About our family. They will be incomplete. Opaque." He lowered his head. "Just give me a chance to explain it before you let anger take you."

Ed said nothing.

Benefactor looked at him again. "Our family is subject to a vendetta. Heathren called it a curse, but it isn't born of fate. It's malice driven by an enemy. One who has known me for most of my life. Heathren belongs to his clan. This enemy has his hands in much. Dread Corps answers to him. He manipulates the Holy Alliance and all the Nether Realms." The Leader of the Grells worked his jaw for a moment. "I cannot tell you his name. Not yet. And I cannot say why."

Ed kept his mouth shut, though anger simmered at the edges. He wanted to rant at his grandfather, but he already did that in his head with hundreds of other reactions, using his training to think through downstream effects at hyper speed. And this stoic silence was the best avenue to get any sort of elaboration.

His grandfather filled in the silence. "There are costs to defying this enemy. And I have recently paid them, along with this world. The War of No Hope. He sent Dread Corps to terrorize the world for decades as punishment for an action I took."

That broke Ed's will to maintain a dispassionate wall. "The whole war? Not just the attack that killed Mom?"

Benefactor nodded.

"What did you do?"

"I tried to tell someone else his name."

Ed swallowed hard, inferring what his grandfather did not say. This enemy had power. Vast amounts of it. The cause of his parents' and his grandfather's secrecy suddenly made a lot more sense. "So how do we fight him?" He remembered one of his mother's last words, not vengeance. Another one. A better one. "How do we win?"

"We can't. Not without leverage. Without resources. Without allies. We're getting closer. You will help us with that. And he knows it. Which will make things worse, but we will rise to the challenge." Benefactor clasped Ed's shoulder. "This conversation happened in real time. You're ready to leave the Sphere."

Ed nodded. "Already figured out today was the last day in here." He beamed. "I'm going to run in the sky. Really, really fast. Then I'm going to ram my fist down this enemy's throat."

"In due time." Benefactor pointed his finger upward. "I'll clear the air traffic for your victory lap. You deserve it."

He lowered his hand and clasped Ed's shoulder again, a little tighter this time. "But your training is not yet completed. You have a few years under Een's and Flynn's tutelage in front of you."

Ed popped his lips. "Yeah, I know." He looked around the Sphere with a mix of nostalgia, awe, and weariness. Vick had made this place years ago, knowing Ed would need it. They conceived him and his brother to be hyper-powered warriors to win against adversaries, both seen and unseen. His family had been preparing for Ed and Matt's lives for decades, perhaps centuries, before they took their first breath. "Can you ever tell me everything about this enemy?" He remembered something else Heathren said. "About broken rules?"

Benefactor's eyes widened a bit at that. He then nodded. "Conditions have to be met. Conditions I cannot tell you." His face grew stern. "And tell no one of this discussion. Your father already knows. As do the rest of the Forever Guard. We've told your brother as well. I repeat. Discuss it with no one else."

"I already hate this."

Benefactor released his shoulder and gave him a crooked grin. "Try living it for a few thousand years. Then talk to me about what you hate."

CHAPTER 16

Two Years Later:
The Late Morning of Trires 49th, 1594

Ed bobbed his ankle crossed over his knee with hands crossed behind his head in the short, green grass. He gazed at the cloudless sky. The air seemed lighter. It tasted sweeter. The long years of training were at last over. All the sword play, studying tactics, testing the limits of his powers, all of it was at last behind him.

Fern kicked his foot off his knee, looming down on him from above, casting a shadow over Ed. "You just gonna lay there all day? This is the first time the four of us have been together without other people telling us what to do in forever." He made a thrusting motion with his hand, like he held a sword. "Come on. Get up and show us Bluestreak."

Ed grinned at his childhood friend. He bucked up to his feet in a fluid, practiced motion. He then reached forward, grasped something unseen in the thin air, or more specifically, hidden in a spatial sheath. His arm pulled forth Bluestreak. "That better?"

"Very." Fern leaned in closer. "Damn, that is a nice hunk of metal."

The sword twinkled in the daylight. Ed shifted the sleek azure hilt of the sword in his grip. The narrow, double-edged blade left an eerie, glowing trail, even in this minor movement. The flawless vamberg weighed as much as a feather. Ed still hefted it with great effort. Kindra died protecting him with that sword. Now, with his training at an end, he would use it to honor her memory. Take her place as part of the Forever Guard.

Ed wove a glowing infinity pattern with the sword, watching the water of the Calinar Canal flowing five feet in front of him. To his left, Tamona sightlessly gazed beyond the glowing trail left by the sword, across the other side to the hundred-foot wide canal.

The blue design remained when he lowered his sword. It glittered in the moist morning air.

"I love that trail of light thing it does." Fern crouched down, grabbed a little rock, and tossed it across the top of the slow-flowing canal. It skipped four times before descending into the glimmering current that reflected this daystar's light. "It's like looking at one of those firework sparklers they sell in Beo."

"But brighter." Matt paced along the tall grass of the waterway's shore in a meandering circle, jotting notes in a miniature notebook. The shadows of the lush trees of the park at their rear passed over his newly grown, mustache-free beard.

The gleaming infinity symbol slowly dimmed. Ed glanced to Tamona. "Can you sense Bluestreak's light?"

Tamona shook her head. Unlike Ed, Matt, and Fern, she did not wear casual attire. She wore loose-fitting white clothing with a scarf encircling her head. A red sash armband wrapped around one of her biceps.

"We'll shut up about it then." Ed waited for her to respond as Bluestreak's light disappeared to nothing in the lingering moments. He spoke again when it was apparent she was not going to say anything. "Sorry about that."

"It's okay, Ed." Tamona's voice carried a distant, sober heaviness.

Ed moved in front of her blind gaze. "Something else is bugging you."

She made no reply, wearing her blank expression as a mask.

Ed looked at her armband, then back to her statuesque face. "You're staring at the future and it scares you." He raised the flat of Bluestreak between their faces. A ribbon of light followed it. "I know the feeling, believe me."

"I do. I can detect it frothing from you like steam from a boiling pot." Tamona spoke with a muted tone, like she was afraid to give her words more volume for fear of losing control of them. "We've both been through our own crucibles."

Fern was about to toss another stone when he pivoted on his feet to face her and Ed. "You've always been close lipped about your training in Mun'la. Feel like sharing?"

She raised an eyebrow. "Only if you do."

That did not elicit another quip from Fern, as Ed had expected. Instead, the insatiable joker gave Tamona a bemused smirk.

Ed looked between them, not understanding what had just happened. "Uh, did I miss something?"

"Yes," Matt said. He placed his notebook and pen in a pocket of his brown leather jacket. He stared at Fern and Tamona with his perpetually bloodshot eyes. "Can we skip the part where you play dumb? I've figured all of it out for Fern. And some of it for Tamona."

Fern tossed the rock over his shoulder. It loudly plunked into the Calinar Canal. "In my defense, I was playing dumb, so Ed didn't feel like he was the only one."

Ed smirked at Fern. "One. You're an asshole. Two. What are you all talking about? Seriously."

Fern held up a finger. "I contest that insult, chumley. I'm too snazzy to be an asshole. Too dashing." He then swept his hand toward the vacant park behind him. "And since your swarms of fans emptied the park, the second you and Matt set foot in it, I think now's the time to get our fastest slow-wit up to speed."

He gave Ed a toothy, insincere smile. "See, that's a better insult."

Ed raised his eyebrows. "You're ugly and no one loves you."

Two quick strides brought Fern in front of the younger Burnhelt brother, grinning wide. "Tammy–"

"Tamona," she corrected.

Fern's eye twitched in irritation at her correction. "Would you mind holding Ed's fancy sword for a moment?"

Ed extended Bluestreak to her, hilt first.

She cracked the slightest of smiles as she grabbed the handle. She lowered it to her side with a luminous ribbon following its movement. "Not at all."

Ed lashed his arms around Fern's neck in a headlock. He forced Fern to double down under his weight. Fern, in the meantime, wrapped his arms around Ed's thigh. They both fell to the grass, grappling and laughing.

Their rolling wrestling match stopped when they bumped into Matt's calves at the shore. He stumbled forward and fell. Anyone else would have landed in the water. Matt instead levitated in the air with his hyper powers. Ed and Fern broke their respective holds on each other. They regarded the elder Burnhelt brother with apologetic faces.

Matt just gave them a long-suffering glare. "Finished?"

Ed stood up and dusted himself off. Tamona gave him back Bluestreak, and he placed it back in his spatial sheath that was permanently suspended in front of him. "Yeah."

Fern sprang to his feet, his clothes covered in grass stains. "Never. Your brother and I are enemies for life. We're obligated to drag you down with us in the quagmire."

Matt shook his head with the consternation of an elder sibling. He set his feet back down on the grass before the canal. He titled his head upward. "I've just created an Unnotice hex around us. We can talk freely." He gestured to Tamona. "Let's start with you."

She held up a hand. "You're going to say that you've deduced that I was born for a purpose just like you and Ed." She raised an eyebrow. "And also Fern."

Tamona leveled her sightless gaze at Matt. "You put it all together through observation, through research, through thinking. You amaze me. Always have."

Ed and Fern shot each other a glance, neither saying a word.

Tamona snapped a finger. "Don't either of you dare start."

Fern started anyway. "He's got a girlfriend already, Tammy."

"Tamona," she corrected. "Unless you'd prefer that I use your other name. Fernallus."

Ed raised an eyebrow at that. He'd never once heard anyone call Fern as Fernallus. He didn't know that was his friend's full name.

Fern just shrugged. "Go ahead. Cat's coming out of the bag anyway."

She worked her jaw for a moment. "You're insufferable."

Matt looked at Ed, obviously waiting for him to chime in. Ed just held up his hands. "I'm waiting for you to say more, Matty. I can wait to say that we all love Fern anyway." He grinned. "Oh, wait. I already said it. Spoiler."

Matt blew out a sigh and pinched the bridge of his nose. "Everyone finished?"

Ed nodded.

Fern shook his head. "Never."

Despite his apparent irritation, a grin crept along Matt's lips. As much as he pretended otherwise, Ed knew he enjoyed their silliness. So did Tamona. She glared at Fern, but she failed to hide her own tiny smile.

"So," Matt said. "Tamona was born for a purpose like us. I walked in on our mothers talking about it when we were little. It stuck with me, and I researched Chan'lavian rites of passage. You trained in Mun'la at a far younger age than Ed and I started our training. That wasn't unusual. But something else was."

"I trained alone without guidance, but knowing what I needed to practice nevertheless."

Matt nodded. "I discovered that after asking around."

She gave Matt a far more apparent smile. "And you put more together. My Perceptia and my blindness. The former far more acute than any other Chan'la. The latter completely unheard of. Save for Muné."

"Right." Matt gazed at a distant, well-pruned tree for a few seconds. "So what were you born to do?"

"To bring Muné back one way or another," she whispered in reverence. "Starm and his lackeys hold her body in the pico realm of Inparadis." She clutched a fist in front of Matt. "I will free her one day when we have the capability to do it. I still have more years of preparation in Mun'la ahead of me. But once I'm finished, you three will help me. My mother conceived me for that purpose in lagoons of Lake Divinity as other Chan'la are conceived. She timed it with Vick and Kindra's conception of you, Matt." She lowered her fist and swept her open hand in Fern's direction. "But I wasn't the first."

Fern just crossed his arms. "Nope. That'd be me." He glanced to Matt. "And for what it's worth, I let you figure it out. Shifting my eyes yellow when I knew you were giving me a side glance. Eating that whole roast that one time."

Matt gave his newly bearded jaw a brief stroke. "Leaving behind a scale in the shower when I was getting in next."

"Yep."

Ed furrowed his brow. "Scale? Yellow eyes?"

Matt stepped closer to Fern. "Why leave the clues for me, but not Ed?"

"Because I knew you'd just go into researcher mode and talk to me about it years later." He jabbed a thumb at Ed. "This guy would have just asked me pointblank about it when we were kids. Vick asked me to keep it under my hat until you both had manifested your hyper powers and had them under control. But I knew you would be less resentful if I dropped you some hints long in advance. Ed will get over it in a minute or two." He lifted his hand and made a twirling motion. "And here we are."

Ed burned through several dozen responses in his mind within a second and landed on the most obvious one. "So what are you?"

Fern spoke his next words with a casualness inverse to their actual gravity. "I'm a Dragon."

Ed's jaw sagged. He tried saying something, but he couldn't summon the breath to give it voice.

"I am glad you finally said it out loud." Tamona held out a hand, caressing something unseen in the air. "My mother made me keep it to myself when I visited. You have no idea how much I wanted to tell you I knew."

"Prove it." Ed stepped right in Fern's face, looking into his amber eyes. "Show us what you really look like. Show us your true form."

Fern raised his hands up defensively. "Ed, it's still me. I'm still your friend."

Ed pointed at Fern. He wanted to cycle through his choice of words again, but anger bled through, getting the better of him. "Show us!"

"Settle down, Ed." Matt forced himself between them, locking his bloodshot brown eyes with those of his brother. "He's still Fern."

Ed backed away from Matt. "Just show us."

"You'll want to give me a little room."

Ed, Tamona, and Matt backed away from him. Ed tensely grit his teeth when Fern nodded that they had moved far enough.

Fern's body took on a red hue. His clothes melted into his skin as his size doubled, then tripled, then quadrupled. His neck grew long and serpentine. Leathery wings unfolded from his back. His hands and feet became clawed. A lengthy tail grew from his lower back. His jaws elongated into a reptilian muzzle. A pair of white horns grew from the top of his head, pointing backwards. His eyes were slitted and golden now. He looked down at them, now covered in smooth, red scales. His shadow enveloped them all. "This is me."

Ed and Matt looked up at him with slacked jaws. Tamona continued staring forward, unawed by the transformation. Fern fully opened his wings, which spanned at least forty feet. "And does it ever feel good to stretch."

The two Burnhelt brothers continued to look at him. Neither said a word.

"You feel less... compressed." Tamona blindly stared forward at his leg. "What color are you?"

Fern looked at the back of his clawed hands as his wings folded at his back again. "Red, well, more of a light burgundy, or crimson. Yes, I think it's crimson. What would you say, guys?"

Ed now paced around in a meandering circle, utterly stupefied. Matt just kept looking at him.

"Come on, guys. Remember when Ed lifted a hundred and twenty tons for the first time? That was more freaky than this."

Ed stopped pacing when he reached Matt's side again. He popped his lips. "I was wrestling on the ground... with a Dragon."

Fern's tail tethered closer to his feet. "We were both holding back. You're stronger than me. I can't lift one-hundred-twenty-plus tons. Just eightyish."

"Just eightyish," Ed repeated.

Fern crossed his scaly arms. "You don't have anything to be afraid of, guys."

Tamona approached him and ran her hand over his smooth-scaled tail. "They are not afraid of you, Fernallus. They are just taken aback. As am I. You are magnificent."

Fern stooped down to eye both brothers with an irritated frown. "Well, suck it up, suckos. It's still the same old Fern you've always known."

Ed stared into his friend's yellow eyes. He realized he had seen this Dragon before. "You fought Dread Corps with Een, Dad and... Mom."

"Yeah," Fernallus said after his frown diminished. "I was there with you. I just couldn't tell you."

"You tried to save Mom with Een and Dad." Ed bit his lip for a moment. "At least *you* did something."

Fern slowly extended an enormous clawed finger toward Ed's shoulder. Ed didn't flinch away. He let Fern place it on his shoulder. "It's not your fault she died, buddy. We all did everything we could."

Ed patted the Dragon's enormous knuckle. It felt far smoother than he expected, like a polished gem. They all knew whose fault it was. Heathren. Ed clenched his jaw. Actually, perhaps they didn't know. The unnamed enemy of whom Benefactor spoke in the Sphere. Heathren was part of his clan. That was a secret he couldn't reveal. Not yet, at least.

Matt rubbed his fingers over his bearded chin again. "You were always fidgety too. It must have driven you crazy to be stuck in one shape all the time."

Fern looked at the sky. "Yeah, a lot."

"Turn into a gnat," Ed said.

He pulled his finger back from Ed's shoulder and gave Ed a blank stare. "I can't turn into *anything*. I'm limited to other biological species no smaller than a child and no larger than my true form."

"That fits with when Dad brought you home to us." The younger Burnhelt brother looked away to a few of the trees swaying in a gentle breeze. "How old are you really?"

"Twenty-eight," Tamona answered as she walked next to his tail, gliding her fingers over it. "Eight years older than Matt and me. Ten older than Ed."

A tiny plume of smoke ebbed out of Fern's nose. "Okay, that's a little annoying."

The Chan'la grinned. "Good."

Ed turned back to Fernallus. "Why did our Mom and Dad take you on as a ward?"

"My parents made arrangements with your family. They couldn't raise me themselves. They gave me to Vick and Kindra right after I was born. I mean *right after*. And before you ask, yes, I can remember that far back."

"Why could they not raise you themselves?" Tamona asked.

Fernallus arched a hairless eyebrow. "What, your Perceptia didn't tell you that too?"

Tamona stopped tracing her hand over his tail. "Some questions should be asked."

Fernallus shifted his tail away from her. The grass beneath it was completely flattened. He shut his eyes for a time. "I'm going to just show you. It'll be better for you to see it." He gave Tamona an apologetic glance. "Or sense it."

She gave him a friendly nod.

Fern's body compressed inward in moments, and he resumed his Human guise again. However, he changed his eyes from amber to brown, and his hair was now auburn red and far shorter, buzzed close to his scalp. "I'll connect us with a Distance Door."

"What's with the new eye color and hair?" Ed asked.

"You have no idea how boring it is to fake grow hair at Human speed. It's much more fun to switch it up to fit my mood. Get used to that. I'll be doing it all the time."

Ed just shrugged. "That will be a little easier to get used to than the whole turning into a giant reptile thing."

Fern nodded. "Fair point." He gestured with his hand and whispered something. A rectangular portal opened in front of them. It led to long, rusty-red grass rather than the short green variety upon which they currently stood. "Let's go somewhere familiar."

Ed, Matt, and Tamona followed Fern through the Distance Door. They left Ruby's urban, but idyllic, park for a place Ed instantly recognized. His family's old residence on the Red Plains outside of Ruby. Their old house still stood, long since repaired but vacant. No one wanted to resume their residence in this house following Kindra's death.

Still, the house didn't seem foreboding or haunted. Its windows glimmered in the daylight. The roof's double peaks always made Ed think of a friendly letter "M" with windows for eyes. He recalled playing with Matt and Fern inside and outside this place, this home. He remembered his parents laughing. Stretching out in his bed in the morning listening to the sounds of nature outside the open window. The old house held more fond nostalgia for Ed than painful memories. That heartened him.

Fernallus pointed at the ground below the house. "There's a reason your parents built this house here in the middle of nowhere. You all have ways of peering through matter. Take a look about two-hundred feet below the foundation. You'll see something."

Ed's vision shifted first into the electromagnetic spectrum as he peered at the ground. Using a combination of X-rays and infrared, he found a cavern, a big one, as big as an amphitheater. However, X-rays couldn't penetrate it, and infrared just detected a slightly higher temperature than the surrounding soil. He shifted to the Haloi wavelength, and saw a green tinge, meaning that life was present within it. No other spectrum revealed anything.

A glowing blue ring hovered over Matt's eye like a monocle. He frowned in concentration. "Something is blocking electromagnetism and etherea. What is it?"

"A lair of Dragons," Tamona whispered.

Fernallus nodded. "What can you sense?"

"Air. Entering and exiting lungs. Enormous lungs. I can barely hear it, even with my Perceptia. I wouldn't have heard it had you not directed me to do so. There's a potent Unnotice Hex surrounding it. No physical entrances or exits."

The Human-shaped Dragon nodded yet again. "This is where my parents and the rest of my clan slumber. They fled here right after the Eruption. While Vick, Benefactor, and thousands of others were maintaining the massive Q-Field that kept the Flame of Tumult from engulfing New Grelland. They came here because it was safer than any other place else on Trojis for them."

Ed looked away from the ground, still unable to see inside the impenetrable underground sanctuary. "What exactly happened to them? Everything I've read just mentions that they were defeated above the Great Caldron."

"Starm and his followers created a plex hex. It binds all Dragons in Trojis to his will. They must either serve him, or their power is depleted to basically nothing. It took everything they had to get here. They slumbered for centuries, building up a meager reserve of stamina. Some of my kin used it to provide insight to the Grells and the Chan'la. My parents. They used their strength to have me. I'm not subject to Starm's plex hex. I'm free of it. Free to help my family's friends. And one day, help break the plex hex that binds them."

Matt took a few steps through the tall grass. He put his hands in his pockets. "So *our* parents built this house for your sake. To keep you close to them. To stand guard."

Fern looked at the ground. "That's right. We actually thought Dread Corps attacked because they had found them and wanted to dig them out. Until Heathren... did what she did."

Matt looked around. "This is under surveillance by our side, isn't it?"

"Oh, yeah." Fern waved at nothing with a grin. "Vick and Benefactor probably got an alert as soon as we set foot here. I told them I'd bring you here once you knew I was awe-inspiring and worthy of your adulation."

Ed walked next to Matt, then turned back to Tamona and Fern. He wanted to be cross at Fern for keeping this secret, but he couldn't. This was still his old friend. That hadn't changed. "Well, at least we're in this 'born with a higher purpose' thing together."

"Partly together," Tamona said. "I still have much training in front of me with my sisterhood. I'll visit when I can."

"Damn," Fern said. "I was going to suggest a group hug, but now it just feels wrong with the girl ditching us for the popular kids."

She smirked at him, but her face maintained its fond demeanor. "You're such an asshole."

"You really are," Matt said. "Accept it."

Fern looked over to Ed. "Little help?"

"I'd rather help them." Ed bobbed his eyebrows. "Asshole."

Fern broke out laughing. Ed joined in. Matt just grinned. Tamona shook her head, but gave them a gleeful smile.

CHAPTER 17

One Minute Later:
The Late Morning of Trires 49th, 1594

Ben let out a long sigh. One of relief. He, Vick, and Een watched his grand-sons and their friends on a Scrying Sphere deep inside his private library. "Inane jokes aside. This is good. Fern and Ed can join the Forever Guard now. Train further with their full capabilities. We'll need to announce Fern's nature to our military. Discreetly."

Vick paced around the rectangular table with the Scrying Sphere floating above it. Ben had since muted the sound. Neatly arrayed oaken bookshelves flanked the table with their many leather, vellum, wood, and paper spines facing them. They towered twenty-five feet above them with a few ladders hanging upon wheels and guiding metal grooves. Many more rows were aligned with their ends facing them, making a series of cozy aisles. "We need to normalize them with the officers. People are afraid of them. You saw how they left the park."

Ben tapped his chin, watching Fern breathe a flaming circle in the air in front of Tamona, who reached her hand through it with a guilty smile. "You aren't wrong. Dragons have been only enemies for a very long time. And Ed's powers are very–" Ben paused as Ed fanned the fire away with a spiraling motion of his arm that moved faster than rotor blades. "Overt."

Een pressed her hands against the table, scrutinizing the four youths on the glowing orb. "I'll cycle them through meeting all the Grellish officers and enlisted personnel. Bring in several Chan'la leaders while I'm at it. Make them familiar. Endearing. Their jokes actually might help with that."

"Entirely possible." Ben inhaled the library's rich aroma of paper. The many preservation hexes had long prevented the acidic degradation of the older tomes. He liked to breathe it at moments like these. When he needed to contemplate many things at once. "Ed is a Burnhelt. Our name will help a bit with his case. With Fernallus, we will need to convince the officers and other leaders that he's unique. He isn't *a* Dragon. He's *our* Dragon."

"Plus, he's an asshole," Vick said. "Plenty of those in the military, so he'll fit in fine."

Ben just gave his son a wry expression. "Indeed."

Een jabbed an elbow in Vick's ribs. "They get their sense of humor from you, you know."

Vick twitched, though not from her elbow.

Ben repressed the urge to laugh, both at the Chan'la's true words, and also at Een and Vick's casual familiarity. They still had sex on occasion. He could tell by the way Een looked at Vick, and the way his son pretended not to notice. Given his son's unease with her playful hit, it was infrequent and not beyond anything casual. And that was for the best. All three of them were painfully aware of Corsis's vendetta against any Burnhelt's romantic interests.

Vick shook his head, heedless of Ben's inner observations. "Honestly, I think Fern was the one who rubbed off on the boys. He started making jokes literally from day one."

"That he did," Ben said in a muted voice. Fern was not the only merry soul. Ben recalled making jokes of his own with Gath and Xax long ago. With Veloc and Selene. With Corsis. He pushed that errant line of thinking away. "At any rate, we are getting closer to it. Our enemy. He will not stay hidden much longer. He will act through the Alliance, Sufrinzon, Dread Corps, or others."

"Or all of them," Vick said, his face now grim.

Ben nodded. "Yes." He gestured to Ed and Fern. "Get those two as much time in the Fire Well as possible. It will hone their skills."

Ben then pointed to Matt. "The elder brother. I'll continue to school in mancy and strategy."

The Leader of the Grells lowered his hand when he took in Tamona. She looked just like Muné now. "She already knows what she needs to do."

Een regarded her daughter with a far more critical eye. "She does, but she's reckless about it. She likes to skip to the end of things. I'll need to break her of that if others in my sisterhood cannot."

Ben nodded, doubtful anyone would succeed in changing Tamona's temperament. In that, she differed from Muné. The slain goddess had been more reserved, somewhat withdrawn when she wasn't in public, borderline reclusive, though less so with her friends.

The ancient warrior dearly wished he could just take a decade off. Just relax. Not have the weight of this world and so many others on him. He clenched a fist, knowing he couldn't relent. Not now. Dear gods, he just wanted to tell Ed, Matt, Fernallus, and Tamona about the Game. About Corsis.

That, of course, would be catastrophically unwise. Corsis directed Dread Corps to attack the entire super continent with the War of No Hope in response to Ben's attempt to tell Starm of the Game. He also forbade Ben from leaving New Grelland ever again, or face worse consequences. At some point, the Game's rules would need to be broken if they were to ever defeat Corsis. For now, he had to abide by their enemy's restrictions and Play the Game.

As did everyone else. Whether they knew it or not. He gestured to the four young ones on the Scrying Sphere. "Perhaps you two should go speak with them. Give them some advice."

Een shook her head. "They can get that later. They need time by themselves right now." She gestured to the door. "As do you. Come on, Vick."

Een's Perceptia had been Kindra's dying gift bequeathed to her. It wasn't as sensitive as that of Tamona, but the mother Chan'la used it well. "Thank you."

Vick nodded to his father before they departed Ben's library, walking past the bookshelves with antiquated tomes, maps, optical disks of varying types, and the occasional hologram display. His son and the Chan'la closed the door behind them, leaving Ben alone with his thoughts.

The Leader of the Grells banished the Scrying Sphere with a flick of his hand. He then meandered down an aisle, this one containing cracked leather books that had once belonged to Cora Burnhelt, his mother. She went mad before his father slew her. Driven insane by the Eavae.

That was the beginning of it. Starting with Xax saving Gath, failing to do the same for Rick Burnhelt, Ben's father. And ending with Corsis outsmarting

Mekem. Everything stemmed from the events of the Weird War over four-thou-
sand years ago. Most notably, most tragically, Corsis making the Weird Ones'
Game his own.

He turned a corner, and his jaw clenched. Corsis stood behind one of his
tables, looking down at a map of Old Grelland.

The Master of the Game did not appear in the reptilian guise with which
Mekem had cursed him. He wore his original appearance, that of a svelte but
sturdy man with blonde hair, amber eyes, and a broad grin. That grin once
comforted Ben with its steady confidence. Far different feelings stirred at the
sight of it now.

Ben pulled a book from the end of the nearest shelf and threw it at Corsis. It
passed through the intruder's body and its leather cover slapped another table,
slid across it, and hit the floor with a clomp.

Corsis gave him a half-lidded stare. "Really, Bennet? Again?"

Ben stood rigid, regarding the man who had directly or indirectly killed
billions, including his wife and his son's wife. The megalomaniac tormented
billions more from the shadows. "Verification of your presence."

The Master of the Game sighed. "Someday. It might really be me standing in
your midst."

A glowing vamberg appeared in Ben's hand, Alabast. "Say whatever you need
to say."

Corsis moved a foot back in a more relaxed pose, his black and red robes
swayed behind him. "Oh, I *need* to say nothing. It's more what I *want* to say."

Alabast grew brighter as Ben focused more ethereal power in the summoned
sword. "Spit it out."

"I'm putting in the screws soon, old friend." He waited a beat. "What? No
correction? No statement that we aren't friends?"

Ben wanted this over, and arguing about their old friendship would just set
this egomaniac on a tirade about their glorious days on the same side against the
Weird Ones. Ben continued to focus more of his power into Alabast, readying a
plex hex. A very particular one that he updated and improved with every passing
year. "You were saying something about screws."

Corsis's smile diminished a bit. "Yes. It's going to get worse. Ultimately, as
bad as the Eruption. And it will be most entertaining."

Ben looked down at his glowing sword, then over to a far bookshelf. He still had a letter Corsis had sent him long ago, long since folded within the pages of a particular index of Grellish laws in another aisle. He recalled the first line of it often. "Nothing pleases you more than entertainment."

That made Corsis blurt out a laugh. "That is true." His illusory form took a few steps through the table. "And I will not be denied. If you break Rules, it will be the end of you. I promise you that."

Ben remained quiet, still building the power within his sword.

"Do you understand?"

Ben nodded.

"I don't believe you."

Ben didn't respond.

"You think this time will be different." Corsis's face tightened. Ben knew the façade of his amicable antagonism was about to melt away, exposing the Archmancer's far more hostile and true nature. "You think the New Players will change things. Your grandsons. Muné's duplicate. The little Dragon. Perhaps Xax. Perhaps others of whom you may or may not be aware." Corsis took another step toward him. "Your thinking is faulty. I am ready for them."

Ben still kept his mouth shut.

Corsis looked from side to side at the bookshelves that flanked him. "I suppose you're going to update your plex hex again. Prevent my remote intrusion." He stormed toward him. His eyes shifted to reptilian slits surrounded by a golden hue. His face went manic. "Know that I can always make you suffer, Bennet. Know it!"

Alabast flashed, filling his library with blinding light. It regressed an instant later. Corsis was gone. Ben's Privacy plex hex had successfully banished Corsis until the next time he cracked it.

"This time will be different, Corsis." Ben grimaced at the spot once occupied by the greatest villain of this long age. Hidden from the gaze of the world, of history. An old friend. His dead sister's fiancé. A man who would have been family. A man who needed to be stopped. "Know it."

THE END of BOOK 3.5
PLAYERS OF THE GAME

AFTERWORD

Now that you know their origins, check out Players of the Game Book 3: The New Players if you haven't already. Join the James McGowan Reader Group at stelfire.com to get notified of all new releases in the series.

Coming soon: Ashe and Avril cross paths with Ed, Harry, and the rest in Players of the Game Book 4: The Breakers. Goddesses must be freed. The Alliance will unleash hell. Corsis will make things worse.

Please also submit a review of this novella. It helps other readers like you find this story.

ABOUT THE AUTHOR

James McGowan lives in Nebraska. In addition to writing, he enjoys enticing his lovely wife with new recipes, though his black bean Marsala pasta is a favorite standby. While writing is his passion, he also likes getting out of the house for walks and hikes. He's always up for a game of pitch with friends too. James is a fan of comic books and often enjoys their adaptations to other media. He's a member of the Nebraska Writers Workshop, the Nebraska Writers Guild, and the Alliance of Independent Authors.

Website: stelfire.com

Facebook Fan Page: JamesMcGowanAuthor

Join the James McGowan Reader Group at stelfire.com

Get a notification email for all new releases in the series at https://books2read.com/author/james-mcgowan/subscribe/1/174474/

www.ingramcontent.com/pod-product-compliance
Lightning Source LLC
Chambersburg PA
CBHW052000170626
46808CB00007B/2703